Every *good* Thing

Every *good* Thing

JOY E. RANCATORE

LOGOS & MYTHOS PRESS
SLIDELL, LA, USA

In honor of the Creative Legacies of
the Rev. Thomas G. Kay Sr. and Mrs. Jane Kay
and in loving memory of them.
My grandparents stoked the spark of a little girl's dream.

They knew how to embrace
Every Good Thing
(*Life Can Be Beautiful ... Believe* THEM!)
and taught that gift to their
children,
grandchildren,
great-grandchildren,
great-great-grandchildren
and on.

"Every good gift and every perfect
gift is from above, and comes down from the
Father of lights, with whom there is no
variation or shadow of turning."
James 1:17

Other Works

Fiction

Carolina's Legacy Collection:
Any Good Thing: A Novel
This Good Thing: A Novella
Every Good Thing: A Short Story Collection
One Good Thing: An Epistolary

The Crux Anthology
"Ealiverel Awakened"
Edited & Compiled by Rachael Ritchey

Nonfiction

Finders Keepers: A Practical Approach to Find and Keep Your
Writing Critique Partner
Joy E. Rancatore and Meagan Smith

Table of Contents

Each of the characters in the following short stories played big or small roles in *Any Good Thing* and *This Good Thing*, previous publications in Carolina's Legacy Collection. This list reminds readers who they are and how they featured in those storylines.

"Miracles & Catfish"

Earl and Eileen Haney appear briefly in *Any Good Thing*. Readers of the novel may remember Eileen best as Memaw and probably still salivate over thoughts of her famous catfish with a side of hushpuppies dipped in cheese sauce.

"Preachers & Roses"

Rev. Benjamin Burns serves a vital supporting role in both *Any Good Thing* and *This Good Thing*. As pastor of Bellum Baptist Church and counselor at Damascus Road Mission, a local mission for recovering addicts, Ben guides others to find the right path.

"Books & Dreams"

Becky Calhoun is Jack's mama. She nearly didn't have her voice in *Any Good Thing*. Thanks to the insistence of a wise critique partner, Becky spoke; and her mother voice greatly improved the novel and *This Good Thing*.

(This story is dedicated to Mea who donned boxing gloves for Becky. Please always fight for my characters!)

"War & Peaches"

Fast-talking, worrying, loving **Mawmaw Mabel Miller** has a fixation on butter, pinochle and constant chatter. Readers might remember her from *Any Good Thing* as an award-winning dumplin' and biscuit maker.

"Love & Cummerbunds"

Hands down, **Patrick "Ducky" Miller III**—the COO of Miller Construction, son to Pat Junior, grandson to Senior and Mawmaw Mabel, boyfriend/fiancé/husband to Daisy and friend to Jack—is the *Any Good Thing* character who elicits the strongest reactions from readers. Thankfully, most are incredibly positive.

"Life Lessons in Courage & Woodworking"

As the main character of *Any Good Thing*, **Jack Calhoun** overcomes much adversity while processing internal conflict and walking through a life filled with lessons. His story here showcases several other supporting characters from his book.

"Joy of Forgiveness"

Jaida Masters might be considered the most unlikely recovering alcoholic in Jack's counseling group at Damascus Road Mission in *Any Good Thing*.

"Look of Promise"

Shannon Ryan Savage survives trafficking, overcomes addiction and chooses a future for herself and her daughter after graduation from the Damascus Road Mission in *Any Good Thing*.

"Life of Purpose"

Pete Sanford is Jack's roommate at the Damascus Road Mission. He tells Jack in *Any Good Thing*, "You'll have people enter your life that'll be more of a support than you might think. Some are there for a few minutes; others decades. Each has a reason for meeting you when they do. Look for those reasons and thank God for 'em."

"Pride, Burned"

Jed Ross appears briefly in the homeless community in *Any Good Thing*. Scarred and armless, Jed thanks Jack for Ducky's number and plans to call him for help in returning his family to an actual home.

"Absence, Reflected"

Anna Claire Clarkson loses her love (and father of her son), Steven Goodtime, on the night of the tragic accident that opens *Any Good Thing*.

"In-Between Moments"

Grandma Ethel Henry becomes everyone's grandma in *Any Good Thing*, though Jack's sniper buddy Trayvon is her only biological grandchild. Her love, care and spoken truths are even more welcome than her sweet potato pie ... and that's saying something.

Discover more about the entire Carolina's Legacy Collection:

Legacy of Faith

"My brethren, count it all joy when you fall
into various trials, knowing that the testing
of your faith produces patience. But let
patience have its perfect work, that you may
be perfect and complete, lacking nothing."
James 1:2-4

Miracles & Catfish

Three years wasn't far enough removed from seminary's book learning to prepare the Rev. Benjamin Burns for what waited in Room 213 of Bellum Medical.

Earl Haney had been admitted the previous day. Moments before the preacher's arrival, the doctor delivered grim news to Earl's wife, Eileen. He then fled, barely avoiding the water pitcher Memaw (as she was known to everyone) hurled at his head.

Memaw made the best fried catfish in a two-hundred-mile radius. On this day, she coated her grief in a thick batter of bitterness. She was scared, angry and ready to fight anyone about to take her Big Love away from her ... God Almighty included. Big Love had been her pet name for Earl since they met forty years earlier, and she intended on calling him that for at least another forty.

God help whoever got in the way of her plan.

Oblivious to the turmoil behind the closed door, Ben clutched a list of patients in his hand and began a prayer for wisdom before knocking for his first solo hospital visit. He hadn't gone far past "Father God …" with his petition when the door whooshed open.

Memaw—all 4 feet 11 inches, 280 pounds of her—nearly plowed over Ben. Her shock at the sight of the Baptist preacher flipped to annoyance that mutated into rage. The Haneys weren't members at his church—or any church, for that matter.

Eileen Haney wasn't big on God. She grew up in Sunday school but didn't see the point when she got older unless they had kids to take. Jesus fit others fine but came across too judgey for her style. Besides, Sunday brought in the most money at her restaurant. She wouldn't miss that.

She snapped at the still gaping preacher, "Well, whaddaya want, boy? You tryin' to catch a fly in that trap of yers?"

Ben stammered, "No ma'am; no fly-catching here, ma'am. Prayer! I'm here to pray. With you. With Earl …"—here he paused to check the now-crumpled sheet in his hand—"Earl … Hiney?"

"That's 'Haney,' boy; and get yer facts straight: Earl don't care for prayin' of any sort. Course, maybe he won't toss you out since yer a kid, and he's got one foot in the grave and the other on a banana peel. He hasn't opened his eyes since we got here."

Her final statement moistened toward the end. Memaw spun on her toes and led Ben into a darkened room, the somber ambiance befitting a gloomy diagnosis.

Ben's lips silently issued a plea to the Almighty for assistance or, preferably, deliverance as he followed Memaw. As Ben would soon discover, Earl was not a small man. Giant feet dangled far off the end of the hospital bed. The preacher's eyes traveled up a mountain range under snowy blankets until they rested upon an enormous head.

The *Guinness Book of World Records* told Earl he could claim the spot of tallest man. When they said they'd send out a photographer, he replied that he'd rather keep his eyesight than get famous. He'd never trusted camera flashes.

Those Book people couldn't believe the luck of finding someone less than a hair under 9 feet and dubbed him "impossible" and "incredible." They called for a while, hoping to add him to their collection.

Earl didn't find his height all that interesting. He'd come to accept his size, but it had always been a bit of a pain to live in a world made for everyone but him.

Memaw neither minded her husband's height nor was she dazzled by it. He was Earl; she was Eileen. They fit together well in most every way. She talked for the both of them. He reached the high stuff; she managed the low. Their devotion outshone any other couple's this side of Eden's fruit.

Earl and Eileen had no biological children, but they'd taken in all the strays for hundreds of miles. Without an official foster situation, kids showed up at the Haney's rambling ranch-style home—lonely, scared, needy. The couple never turned one away, though they got robbed a couple times by a kid gone bad.

The revolving door of the Haney home filled empty hearts with a lifetime of love and expanded their family beyond a traditional size. One of the first teens to call the house his home dubbed Eileen, Memaw, and the title stuck.

Earl was simply Earl to everyone who knew him. He worked with a logging company while Memaw fed her rag-tag army and perfected cooking. After the hundredth kid told her she should open a restaurant, she turned to Earl before they fell asleep in their custom-made bed and informed him she was opening a catfish house. He replied, "It's about time, dear;" and they went to sleep. *Memaw's* opened two weeks later.

Ben would learn the couple's history long after his miracle prayer, as Memaw called it. He inched toward the resting giant.

"I'm sorry to hear Mr. Hi—Haney's doing so poorly, Mrs. Haney. Is there anything I can do for you? Anyone I can call?"

"You can call down a miracle from that God of yers. Doctor says my Big Love's organs are failin', and none of his fancy tests give him a reason or rhyme for it. He can't do a durn thing other than buzz medical terms and grate on my nerves like a dang mosquito."

With Memaw's brusque greeting, the young minister had started sweating. At her request for a miracle, Ben found himself in danger of dehydration.

He did a mental flip-through of all files on miracles from his years in seminary. Water to wine. Demons in swine. He sure wasn't Jesus. He wasn't even one of the Apostles to whom Jesus gave the ability to dole out miracles.

"Well, ma'am, I'd be happy to pray for Mr. Haney, if you'd like me to. I can do that right here. Out loud. If you want." Ben gulped, an audible clue to the state of his nerves.

Memaw squinted at the sweaty man before her. "Boy, I sure hope Jesus has got more patience with yer stammerin' than I do. Get on with it, then. Pray away. You better call him Earl, though. That's the only name anyone knows him by; and I doubt your God's any dif'rent."

Ben bowed his head, inhaled the stale hospital air and muttered a prayer that grew in force and confidence from some reserve of wisdom and courage he'd never before tapped.

"Heavenly Father God, we come to you this afternoon with hearts worn down and burdened with sadness over the condition of Mr. ... of Earl. You've given Earl a full life with his wife here, but I pray, Father, that you would make a way for this to not be the end for them. Make this a beginning—a beginning of something none of us could've ever imagined. I pray, Father God, that you'll heal this man and restore him into his wife's arms. And, God Almighty, I pray that when you do this ... this miracle, make them know it came straight from you. Soften their hearts and make them your dwelling place. Save them from an eternity apart from you. We ask all these things in the powerful name of your Son, Jesus Christ. Amen."

Stunned at the words that had flowed from his mouth, Ben kept his head bowed. He figured the stern woman would be glaring at him and prepared for an attack for his brazenness. Instead, Memaw's face held a gentleness her grief previously covered. Her eyes remained fixed on the bed, and Ben followed her sight line.

Earl gazed back at his bride, his coal black eyes peace-filled. Ben looked from the man to his wife and back again. Tears trickled down their cheeks, and something passed between the couple that defied Ben's interpretation.

"I sure would like one of your catfish plates, Memaw." Earl's rumbling voice startled Ben with its booming normalcy.

The preacher caught the next surprise out of the corner of his eye, but not in time. Memaw barreled around the bed and seized Ben in the tightest hug he'd ever survived. Too tightly wrapped to speak, he patted her back and shifted his gaze to the openly weeping patient.

Eileen's words rose muffled from the face pressed against Ben's chest. "Bless you, Preacher Boy. God spoke through you today and sent a miracle into this room. I've got my Earl back, and I won't soon forget yer words."

"We'll think about comin' to that church of yours once I'm outta this tiny excuse for a bed."

Shock flashed across both Ben's and Memaw's eyes. Earl hadn't expressed a desire to attend church since the Pentecostal preacher told his mama they needed him to play Goliath in the church drama. He declared he was no circus freak for a bunch of religious fanatics to parade about for their storytime. From that day on, he made a wide berth around any church buildings or preacher types.

Earl kept his word to Pastor Ben, though.

The first Sunday morning the Haneys attended Bellum Baptist, God woke Ben at 3 to rewrite his sermon. Ben wasn't in the most preacherly of moods by the time he arrived at church. When he stood to welcome the congregation and spied Earl sitting head and shoulders above everyone, all color drained from the preacher's face.

He wished he had his original sermon about Jesus feeding 5,000 folks with one boy's lunch. It included a joke about how much better southern-fried catfish would have been. All during the hymns and special music, Ben tried to mentally recreate that sermon, but only the passage on the page in front of him whispered back. He couldn't even recall the punchline of his catfish joke.

As soon as Marge Turner hit the high C on her solo, sweat beaded on Ben's forehead, back and upper lip. The oxygen forsook his lungs as he staggered to the pulpit. His voice sounded far away and hollow to him—like a long-distance call with a bad connection.

"Open up your Bibles with me to Mark, chapter 2. I'll read verses 27 and 28 today." He cleared his throat and read, "'And He said to them, "The Sabbath was made for man, and not man for the Sabbath. Therefore, the Son of Man is also Lord of the Sabbath."'"

Ben looked up, locked onto Memaw's steely gaze and clutched the pulpit to keep from going down with his buckling knees. He launched into a homily on man's need for a Sabbath—one day of rest in seven. Despite his best efforts to reign in his honesty, he heard himself condemn work on Sundays and the businesses that forced their employees to miss church. As he squeaked out the last line of the sermon God sent him, Ben collapsed in a dead faint right on the church stage.

He awoke on the couch in the church library to the befuddled expression of Deacon Joe who informed him that the Haneys had come down the aisle when Deacon Pat extended an invitation. They said they were doing what the song commanded—deciding to follow Jesus. The Haneys wanted to join the church, and beginning the next Sunday, *Memaw's* would no longer be open for churchgoers' lunch needs.

In Memaw's words, "You ladies best get out yer roastin' pans to cook lunch while yer singin' praises here."

As unexpected as the outcome of Ben's impromptu sermon had been, the Haney's initial response paled in comparison to Memaw's announcement a month later. She waved a $5,000 check under his nose and dropped it in the offering plate.

"That's how much we made above what we brought in last month. If I'd known shuttin' down on Sundays would be *more* profitable, I'd have done it from the beginnin'."

Memaw patted Ben's arm as he stood before her, mouth agape once more.

"You come on by the restaurant this week with your sweet little wife, and I'll fix yer plates myself. Only the best for my Preacher Boy."

Preachers & Roses

"**D**aggone! Son of a ... monkey's uncle."

Preachers aren't supposed to cuss. The thorns on this rose bush, though, draw unsavory words. Finger to tongue, I taste metal. Not the first time today; likely not the last.

How Carolina didn't stay cut up, I'll never know. She dug all around these prickly plants without a scratch.

I spit in the direction of the offending bush. The mixture of dirt and blood isn't exactly appetizing. I wipe the sweat from my forehead and lean back, arms resting on my knees, to survey Carolina's garden. It's already lost much of its glory since she passed away in September. The butterflies must agree; I haven't seen any yet.

My wife tilled magic in this land. With her fingertips, she commanded the soil and caressed the seeds. Every day she whispered to her plants and bushes. I look at the one before me again ... her favorite—the L.D. Braithwaite—as regal as his name. In her final days, she taught me how to care for this one, and I promised to keep it alive for her. For us.

I close my eyes and smile at the vision she was—rosy cheeks, glowing smile—as she guided my clumsy hands to prune, just so, to water here, not there. Eyes squeezed, I don't want to open them. These days, I can only see her, real and living, when they're shut.

Time has slipped past since she left. When I said goodbye to my better half, my existence stuck on fast-forward, and I want it to stop.

And, I don't. The faster the days go, the sooner I get to join her.

The door slam jerks me from my inner debate, and I watch Rachael dash down the steps. Her smile, her hair, her glow— our daughter is a mini-Carolina, top to toe. For her, I can't let the darkness control me. For her, I must slow life down and focus. At her, I smile.

She stops, hands on her hips, and shoots me that disapproving look that makes me wish I hadn't made whatever mistake has earned her disappointment. Carolina had a similar effect.

"You cut yourself again, didn't you, Daddy?"

From her pocket, Rachael pulls one of a few bandages. I shake my smile at her constant preparedness—one hundred percent her mother, this one.

"You know you have to talk to him; mama always did. You've gotta learn to speak 'Rose' or we're gonna lose him." Ending her lecture, Rachael frowns and nods toward the bush. "I'm going back in for a snack before I finish my homework. I expect you two to figure out how to communicate."

She picks up the bandage garbage, kisses my cheek and returns to the house.

"It seems we've been given an ultimatum, good sir."

If someone had told me I'd talk to a rose bush one day, I would have offered them counseling.

"You have to start talking back if this is gonna get us anywhere."

The leaves rustle, and I feel the breeze on my neck. I remember again Carolina's hands guiding mine—her soft words, the music of her laughter—and I lift the shears. This time, I examine the bush from multiple angles, then feel different spots. Eyes closed, I listen to each.

This one should be cut. Not this one.

I make my way around the plant's circumference, feeling and listening ... sensing. I whisper, not to the inanimate object before me, but to the wife who still lives in my heart, my mind, the core of my being. We were, after all, together for twenty-six years. For sixteen of them, we were husband and wife.

"Carolina, you were always wiser than I could ever hope to be."

Touch. Eyes close. Listen. Open. *Snip.*

"How can I parent our girl without you? I can't answer all the questions she's going to have. She'll be a teenager in less than a month, for goodness' sake."

Touch. Eyes close. Listen. Open. Move on.

"I don't know if I want to keep preaching. Could I serve better focusing on counseling at the mission?"

Touch. Eyes close. Listen. Open. *Snip.*

"I think I'm frustrated with preaching every week to people who, honestly, I'm not sure care what I say or want to discover the depths of God's word. Maybe I just want to run from this place. You know I can run."

Touch. Eyes close. Listen. Open. *Snip. Snip. Snip.*

"Rachael's had enough upheaval. She needs a constant right now. I don't think I should make a big change. Plus, I can continue preaching and do more at the mission."

I set the shears down and plead with God to correct all the mistakes I'm certain I made. As I survey the shrub before me, I worry I cut too much, wonder if it needs more water or food. Then I dust the dirt from my hands and breathe deeply.

"Enough. It's enough for now."

§

March 1999

I'm at it again, watering can in hand. I worry and fret around Carolina's rose, as I have the past couple of years. If I water too much, he'll die. If I water too little, he'll die. Never in a million years did I think I'd feel anxious about a stupid bush.

"If you were here, you'd take this drought in stride. Me? I'm as nervous as a parakeet in a room full of cats."

My habit of talking to my wife while tending her rose continues. These years have shown me how helpless I am. Though nowhere near as vital to my life as prayer, talking to Carolina helps me work through concerns because I imagine her response. When someone's part of another for as long as she was with me, comfort exists even in the memory of her words.

I feel the ground around the rose for the umpteenth time. "That should do it." I set the can down before I lower myself to the nearby bench.

Carolina loved to sit here, surrounded by the scents and sounds of her peaceful garden. Though it hardly looks like her garden now, I know she would understand and even be pleased. I have kept her rose alive.

"That's no small feat, you know, especially with this black thumb."

I hear her laughter roll on the wind and smile at the memory's caress. As the moment fades, I slide off the bench to the ground.

"Rachael and Jack have been riding a dangerous road together. Their relationship, for one thing, has been heating up. When I see the way he looks at her as he slides his hand around her waist …," I clench my fists on my knees as indignation rises in my chest. "Well, it makes me want to hit him upside his hormone-addled head with that baseball bat we bought him for his tenth birthday."

I remember that party. In many ways, it played out the same as the previous nine. Becky brought out the cake she'd baked late the night before after her second job. She set it, candles aglow, in front of Jack. Rachael leaned closer to him as we all sang. He blew out the flames with a wish. Becky cut into the cake and gave the first piece to the birthday boy, who promptly passed it to his best friend—my Rachael.

Every birthday, every holiday, every Tuesday—our kids had been inseparable from birth. Becky and Carolina were best friends before then. When Becky's husband left, I looked for opportunities to spend time with Jack. The bat, ball and glove set we gave him aided my intention.

After his party, I played ball with Jack and Rachael at the park near his house. He taught her to slide into home plate. I got an earful from Carolina when she saw the dirt caked into our daughter's clothes—a talking to I laughed off as I teased and kissed her anger away.

That was life before cancer and before our kids began acting like pseudo adults.

Recently, they've begun attending parties where coolers no longer contain juice boxes. Rachael has started partaking, but I haven't decided how to handle the situation. I brought the issue to Carolina's rose bush more than once but got nowhere near a solution before our world shifted again.

"One week ago, four of their friends died in a drag racing accident. Rachael and Jack were there. He got hurt bad, needed surgery. Thank the good Lord for Dr. Harvey."

I rest my head on the bench behind me; the sun kisses my face. As the memories of that night replay, a cloud passes overhead.

"I got the call and only knew some teens were injured … and some were dead. They didn't tell me who. I'm still not sure how I got to the hospital. The terror of thinking I could lose Rachael, too …"

The tears rise, pumped by my tattered heart. I push away the *what could have beens* and think back to the *what was*.

"Becky sure needed you that night. She was worried sick about her son. Rachael held her while she cried, though."

I picture our friend. I'd only seen Becky cry once before—when we lost Carolina. Thankfully, Rachael had been there with her after Jack's surgery. No one should ache alone.

"You'd be proud of our girl. She confessed she had started drinking, but the accident scared her sober. I've been praising the Lord for that, but I fear the same tragedy kicked Jack further off course. We visited him yesterday. He didn't have much to say—even to Rachael."

The rough bark, scattered out from the rose bush, draws my attention. I tear apart a piece as competing emotions battle within me. Of course, I'm thankful for the positive change I've seen in my daughter, but Jack's been as close as a son to me. He almost died and now ….

"Physically, he's recovering, but I'm not sure how he will mend mentally or emotionally. I ache for him."

Anger rises as I picture my little girl's face last night. She tried to talk to Jack, but he just lay there, his head turned away. I've never seen him like that. Neither has she.

"I watched the joy and hope for Jack's recovery slide down Rachael's face. Carolina, her tears would've broken your heart. You'd know the right words; I don't. I know she's hurting. I have no doubt she loves him. Until our visit, I would have said he thought he felt the same. Now, I just don't know."

Between my fingers, I rub two pieces of bark. I consider the aching hearts around me and focus on the woman who could ease that hurt. Carolina had a way of comforting others that I can never duplicate.

She could also unite people. I think of all she did for Becky. Carolina softened minds that were turned away from the young woman who "wasn't from around here," as Bellum natives would say. She showed how just because a woman's alcoholic husband left her, she's no less of a neighbor. If anything, she's more.

"Becky's breaking." I address the bark residue in my hand. "She'll never talk about it with me, though. Something I haven't mentioned to you before: soon after you passed away—honestly, probably at your funeral—the gossips around here decided Becky and I would be an item. While they seemed to think it was a given and accepted match, they also took it upon themselves to make sure we didn't get up to any mischief."

My one-sided conversation continues as I recount the actions of Bellum's busybodies. "I didn't notice the gossip, but Becky did. We visited often at each other's houses to keep the kids together. She stepped in for a few months to make sure Rachael didn't get overwhelmed with all you'd taught her in the kitchen. My limited culinary ability is no secret."

The clouds shift and tumble, dispersing odd shadows across the yard and into the woods beyond. I contemplate how life moves on, often quicker than we'd like, as our actions touch people around us, with or without our knowledge.

"Anyway, I'm not sure if someone said something to her or if she overheard a not-so-subtle conversation; either way, Becky waited after service one Sunday. Once everyone else had gone, she walked up the front steps of the church and apologized that she wouldn't be spending time at our house anymore. She worried it gave the wrong impression to some church members and didn't want to tarnish my image as their pastor. She hoped it wouldn't upset Jack and Rachael's friendship and said Rachael is always welcome at her home. The dark circles beneath her eyes made me wonder how long she'd been fretting over the situation."

I shake my head and toss more scattered bark toward the rose. A breeze stirs its leaves and wafts its sweetness. I inhale.

When I close my eyes, I see Carolina sitting beside me, her smile certain and uplifting. Her eyes knowing. I feel her touch ... almost. As I open my eyes, earth's reality kicks my chest.

"People's words do so much damage—do they not realize? Do they not care?"

I pull myself back onto the bench as I contemplate unwanted answers.

"My frustration at the church continues. Every Sunday I feel I'm preaching to the pews instead of the people because ... shouldn't people grow if they're listening? I thought again this week about quitting the church and focusing on the mission. Again, I didn't go past thinking to doing and asked myself why. I'm not sure I like my answer. I'm content in the safety of being there. It's comfortable because I've known it for sixteen years. That's a lousy answer. I'm certain you'd wholeheartedly agree and would talk some sense into me ... if you were here."

The creak of the back door announces Rachael's approach. She doesn't bound down the steps as usual. Instead, she trudges beneath her worries. I smile at the child who's growing up too fast.

"Hey, pretty girl!"

A hint of a smile twitches the corners of Rachael's mouth. She sits beside me and rests her head on my shoulder. I kiss her hair and wrap my arm around her shoulders.

"He looks good." She nods to the rose before us.

I laugh. "To be honest, I'm shocked as anything he's still with us."

"Me too."

"Thanks for the vote of confidence!"

Rachael's laughter spreads joy across her face, and I realize how much I needed to see that emotion in her.

"How are you doing with everything?" The question falls, inadequate.

She shifts her braid over her shoulder and fiddles with the tip. "I'm not sure. Everything feels so ... heavy."

I watch her split the unbraided portion of hair evenly into three parts. As she plaits them, her thoughts continue out loud.

"Losing Steven, Leslee, Bobby Lee and Susan doesn't seem real. I never thought I'd go to funerals for four of my classmates."

She undoes her work and tosses the braid to her back.

"And then there's Jack. Daddy, he wouldn't even look at me. Something's not right, and I'm worried. He never drank before that night, but I'm not sure the accident scared him away from it. It might have done the opposite. He blames himself even though he shouldn't. Everyone pushed Steven to race, not just Jack."

As I take my daughter's hand, a teardrop rains on my thumb. I feel the sting of heartache behind it and give her a gentle squeeze.

"I wish I could say something to make you feel better. I wish I could turn back time and change what happened a week ago. What I can do is be here for you and for your friends. You can talk to me any time, and so can they. Do you think Jack will talk to me?"

"He won't even talk to me right now, so I don't know." Rachael's gaze sweeps the now-barren field where Carolina planted a final sunflower surprise for us. "I miss Mama all the time, but I've really missed her this week. Will this ache for her ever go away?"

My own ever-present grief throbs, and I shake my head. "I would love to say yes, but I'm not sure it does. Grief's intensity ebbs and flows, like the tides, but missing her—that's as much a part of us now as the salt is to the ocean."

"I'd rather have her here."

"Me too."

She kisses my cheek and stands. "I'm going to change for the funeral. Anna Claire's going to need me there today. I forgot to tell you: she's pregnant. She didn't get to tell Steven before he died."

Rachael walks inside as I wrap my mind around the bombshell she dropped. I look back at Carolina's rose as the weighty truths Rachael carries sink in.

"We're a mess without you. I wish you were here—like I have every day since you went Home. I miss you more today than yesterday."

§

May 2002

"Not many preachers can say they've delivered a fiery sermon that doubled as a resignation. I'm not sure if you'd be laughing or scolding."

As I rub the silky petals of Carolina's rose, a faintly sweet scent surrounds me. Five and a half years I've kept him alive and well for her. Five and a half years since I touched her skin, held her in my arms, kissed her crimson lips. Five and a half years of missing and loving her so deeply, every breath burns.

"Jack left last night. Wrote a goodbye letter to Rachael." The sun scorches my scalp, and I reach for my garden hat as I consider how Carolina would respond to Jack's thoughtless farewell. "Yeah, I figure you'd have words for him."

I pick a blade of grass and *snap, snap, snap* it before I pick another to repeat the action.

"After all the challenges he's faced and overcome, I thought he was moving forward. He bought our girl a ring. The night of the second accident, I think he was going to propose. Though, he hadn't asked me, which I was a tad annoyed about. Honestly, I have no idea how I would have responded. What would you have said?"

The day's heat stifles any breath that might have whispered on a stray wind.

"They are good together in many ways. I do believe they love each other, but he still isn't walking with Christ. He's come a long way—overcoming some of the guilt he felt after the drag racing accident and getting the help he needed to recover from alcohol's hold."

Jack has been through more than most people twice his age—plus something many would call their greatest nightmare. I would.

"The second accident happened just over a month ago. Old Hiram Cutter—you remember what a hothead he is—stopped Jack on the road that runs through his land. Hiram's had a burr in his butt over some trouble Jack caused his sister while he was still drinking. As I understand it, Hiram hauled back his arm to punch at the kid. Jack's got great reflexes, and he punched the gas enough to pop away from the big man's swing—and enough to run over the girl playing hide and seek by his truck's tire. No one knew Hiram's littlest grandbaby was there."

I stand. Who could sit still with the reflection of such a horrific death? My chest tightens as I imagine how Jack must have felt every day since then. Knowing he was not in the wrong doesn't bring the child back or ease the agony of seeing that tiny lifeless face beneath his truck.

"You remember what a giant of a man Hiram is. Well, to make matters worse, when they realized what had happened, he picked Jack up and threw him into his windshield. I saw the window. All I can say is, I can't believe Jack didn't have more damage than he did. They rushed him to Atlanta because they weren't sure how serious of a head injury he had."

As I circle the rose bed a fifth time, I rub the sweat off my neck and consider the irony of where Jack would have been that night.

"He had been on his way to get Rachael's corsage for their senior prom. Instead of riding in a medevac, he should have been picking up Rachael. Instead of awaiting test results on his brain, they should have been dancing. And, instead of sitting by his bedside, praying he'd wake up, Rachael should have been answering one of the most important questions of her life."

I stop my restless circling and plod toward the tree line. Jack and Rachael played hide and seek in these woods. As they got older, they played chase among the trees. As teens, I caught them leaning against one and sneaking a kiss or two.

Bellum has been their home, their playground and the setting for their coming of age. For Jack, though, it has become his battleground.

It's where his dad left him and his mom when he was little. It's where he made a choice to take a beer and encourage a friend to drag race—a friend who, most certainly, would have taken the challenge presented him whether Jack had egged him on or not. It's where he lost four friends and nearly lost his life. It's where he decided the numbness of alcohol was worth whatever price it demanded of him. It's where the town turned its back on him while he slid further down the slope of addiction and never encouraged him as he trudged up the steeps of recovery. It's where—a year and a month sober—he was in the worst place at the worst time, and a two-year-old died.

I sweep my gaze up the giant pines toward their needled tops, inhale their spice and search for the blue of the sky.

"Bellum will always be the place where people view Jack, not as the kid who's overcome so much hell, but as the drunk's kid who became an alcoholic and leaves death and destruction in his wake. He couldn't bear that future, and so he left."

As I remove my hat, the full force of the sun's rays hits me.

"Carolina, I wish you'd been here last night. I didn't know what to say or how to counsel him. I drove him to the bus station and prayed he'd change his mind, but I knew he was already gone. Yesterday, Hiram's older granddaughter splattered the groceries Jack was getting for Becky all over the checkout counter. His first instinct wasn't to run, though. He went to the liquor store and purchased his old comfort. If I didn't already know how much he's grown, I know now. He recognized the danger, shattered the bottle and took steps to not repeat his mistake."

I move my address from the heavens back to Carolina's rose bush. The sun glistens on the edges of the petals and tricks the light into seeming to originate in the flowers themselves. I recall the battles Jack has fought since the second accident and continue my discourse.

"This town treated him like a leper. Even at Rachael's graduation, people made it clear he wasn't welcome. You'd have known weeks ago what to say to this town about the way they've cast him off and would've said it much nicer than I did. I probably shouldn't have used a sermon to do it or to announce it was my last. At least I finally ended my time as pastor there."

As I walk toward the rose to reclaim my seat on the hard earth in front of the bench, I consider Jack's options.

"Jack could have stayed, of course. He could have talked things through with his mom and Rachael before leaving. The truth is, he didn't think he had the strength to look his mom and girlfriend in their eyes and then leave. All the hatred and blame the town placed on him over the years has convinced him he will continue to be a problem for the people he loves. He explained how the pressure and pain he feels here might drive him back to the addiction he clawed his way out of and swore he'd never return to."

The sigh that rises sticks in my throat. I consider my own options in last night's events.

"That is why he made the choice he did and why I knew I wouldn't change his mind. I chose to be a constant for him as he runs, seeks, struggles. I hope to be there for him when he asks the right questions and pray I speak the answers he needs. I also pray he accepts truth one day soon."

I palm the bits of grass I'd discarded earlier—nature's confetti. Pressing them into my skin, I absently wonder if I'll end up with a green stain. I feel my actions this morning and the strong words I used to condemn the town's inability to love have left a stain on my time as pastor of Bellum Baptist. It wouldn't be the first stain in my past. I reflect on that as I continue expelling my thoughts into the suffocating early summer air.

"Rachael needs you now. I don't know how to comfort her, but you would. You know what it's like to love a runner—through addiction and in recovery. I swear, after all these years, I still kick myself for putting off marrying you, for trying to push you away with college and seminary, for making you wait. You had already waited for me to surrender my life to Christ and to break free of the drugs' hold. I was an idiot—with that, I know you'd agree. What I can't understand is why you waited. What did you see that was worth your devotion, love, understanding and patience?"

Another deep breath fills me with the fragrance of the flower that tethers me to Carolina.

"I fear Rachael's as persistent as you. As stubborn, too." A phantom pain of how Carolina would have repaid my sarcasm stabs my ankle. "I don't want her pining after a guy who may run longer than I did. As much as I love Jack—like a son—I'm not sure how long it might take him to make better life choices, and I don't want him to hold Rachael back anymore. I believe he will come to Christ one day. Rachael believes that, too; she's told me so. The fact is we cannot know for certain. Rachael deserves a solid man of God who loves Him most and her second. A man who's walking toward a future."

The grass remnants drift from my tilted hand and float on the needed relief of a breeze. Through the kitchen window, I watch Rachael and Becky talk as Rachael pulls down glasses, no doubt to fill with the sweet tea she made last night. Since I'm no longer the pastor at Bellum Baptist, we figure tongues can wag however they see fit. God sees all, and He alone can judge. Becky's one of my dearest friends, and my door will always be open to her.

"Rachael and Becky need one another today, Carolina. Becky knew Jack was going to run—she told me that when I gave her the note from him. She said y'all talked about that possibility years ago, too. Knowing doesn't make his leaving easy, though."

I climb the steps onto our deck and cross to a chair. Last night and today have exhausted me more than a typical Sunday. I feel every step of the emotional marathon I've run as I sink into the seat.

"Rachael and I discussed her college options over lunch; I think that's what they're talking about now. That and Jack ... and probably you. They miss you. So do I. Carolina, I struggle to face life without you."

I toss my confession toward the center of our backyard where her stately rose reigns. My eyelids weigh as much as sandbags, and I sink into a time when Carolina sat in the chair beside me while we sipped coffee and talked about everything and nothing.

§

For an instant when I wake, I think my dream transported me back in time. Instead of Carolina, though, her lookalike smiles at me.

"Hey, Daddy."

"Hey back." I'm groggy as I ponder how long I might have dozed.

"Don't worry. You didn't snore or drool or anything."

I laugh. "Thanks. Did Ms. Becky leave?"

"Yeah. We talked about Jack and everything. We kind of get it, but ... mostly, I'm pissed at him."

"I know you are. Saying goodbye in a letter was a crappy thing to do. As your dad, I had a hard time not decking him last night."

"Oh, don't worry! As soon as he comes to his senses, I'm gonna punch him."

Rachael's cheeks flush to match her hair. I almost feel sorry for Jack when I notice the flashes of anger in her bright blue eyes.

In a softer tone, she asks, "He'll come to his senses, won't he?"

As I take her hand in mine, I wish I could scoop away her pain. I don't have an answer to give her and realize that's worse than knowing how much she's hurting.

She brushes away her tears and pulls on a smile. "I feel like writing in my journal, but I'll fix supper after that."

When she stands, I hold onto her hand. "He'll be okay, and he'll figure it out—whatever *it* is." She nods, and I continue. "How about you take a night off cooking, and I'll fix my specialty?"

"Pancakes for supper sounds perfect!" Her smile glows as she bends down to kiss my cheek before entering the house.

Rubbing my hands together, I rise from the chair and return to the rose bush. I've discovered searching for damaging insects can be soothing. The task gives me more time to speak to Carolina aloud, as well.

"We'll take our next steps slowly. I'll follow Rachael's lead. She said she doesn't want to be far away from me for college. I figure wherever she chooses to go will have addicts I can counsel nearby, so the move decision should come from her. I'll remain at the mission until then. It will be a welcome break to have only one job."

Finished with my inspection of the bush, I turn my attention to the soil and push the bark chips around, fingering their roughness. I feel the softness of the earth for adequate moisture. I surprise myself by not needing to think about what the rose did or didn't need. Rose care has become second nature to me.

"I knew the first spring without you, when I learned to talk to you here, I was meant to focus on counseling. You knew that long before I'd even considered it, though, didn't you? I don't know why I clung to the church's security all these years. Comfort can't be the only reason. You'd probably know the truth of that, too, wouldn't you?"

Once more, I give the soil at the base of the plant another touch and relish the feel of the cool earth. I smooth the bark and sit down. Before turning to prayer for guidance, I whisper final thoughts.

"I ache for you, Carolina. Some days the weight of your absence presses me down against the earth in which we laid you. Time will never ease this constriction inside of me that makes it hard to breathe and makes me want to let the darkness pull me under. The thought of leaving this place nearly tears my patchy heart in two, but this place isn't you.

"I've studied how to transport your plant—and I will, though the flowers it produces aren't you.

"You shine and praise in the presence of God. I don't want to run, but I know a move now won't be running *from*. We'll be running *to*—to a new chapter, new opportunities, Rachael's future. God will guide us. I know that. I also know I love you—always will—and that you would be so proud of our girl."

As I switch from conversation to prayer, I smile at the butterflies I hadn't noticed before. They flit on jerky paths from flower to flower. Here for a moment; gone. Back again to land, wings resting then alert, up and down. I thank God for the beauty before me as I watch the sunlight bathe the landscape and feel its rays melt the tension within me.

Books & Dreams

Dreams never belonged to me.

When my Prince-Charming-Come-True walked out on his son and me, I embraced this belief. Thanks to a friendship, a lamp and a book club, I accepted dreams in my life again.

Despite the heavy memory, I feel only today's emotion in the corner of my eye—joy, heavy with the decades leading to this store's opening. Our new flooring holds remnants of the evening's grand opening festivities—dirt, bits of cake, a rumpled napkin or two that tumbled from the overflowing trash bin.

I gaze across my son's handiwork: the low shelves with animal-shaped cutouts, the kiddie table Rachael and I painted, the detailed scrollwork on the floor-to-ceiling bookshelves. I dry my hands on my linen capris before running them along the smooth shelves that uphold my past, present and future.

Many of the books in my shop reside on the literary patchwork quilt of my life. I cast my eyes around, noticing one, nodding to another, laughing with a couple—old friends with whom I share an understanding, a history.

In many ways, books led me to today's dream-come-true—this shop, this beginning. Books also saved me from myself.

Well ... books and Carolina.

Soft light flickers through the glass of a delicate antique lamp nestled in a shelf corner between prairie romances and cozy mysteries.

The flame's glow warms my heart with the memories of my friend I'm left to hold for us both. Many of our most precious moments surrounded this lamp and the books we read by it. My mind drifts into a welcome reminiscence on how the lamp, these books and my family came to this place: *Becky & Jack's*, a shop that combines handmade furniture and books.

Our babies were two years old when Carolina's husband bravely agreed to watch them for us. Ben was—and is—a fabulous friend, husband and father. Carolina and I giggled and fretted about his caretaking abilities and analyzed the barely hidden look of terror he showed on our way out the door.

"He'll be fine! What could a couple of two-year-olds possibly do to a grown man in half a day?"

With that dismissal, we shed our worries and drove to the next county, where we shopped antique row and enjoyed a tantrum-free lunch. That day gifted us something far more lasting than a few hours of relaxation.

The lamp's milk glass base called to me. The roses hand-painted on its glass spoke to Carolina. I can still hear our duet of gasps and feel her garden-worn hand as we pondered the lamp's history and purpose.

"Think of the stories this old lamp could tell!" Carolina's eyes twinkled as she took my hand in hers.

Her joy coursed through her fingertips and into my heart and face. I felt my expression match hers as I said, "Think of the stories that could be read by this lamp's light!"

"Our book club!" Carolina hopped twice with the excitement of her idea. In our hearts, moms are little girls, still thrilled by Once-Upon-A-Times, horses, chocolates and magic lamps.

The first activity we shared as friends was visiting our cupboard-sized local library. That rendezvous naturally led us to sharing favorite books and exploring new ones together. Before we thought to give our chats an official title, we realized we had launched a book club.

Carolina introduced me to the Brontës, and I unveiled my love of western romances like *No Quarter Asked*. We bickered over whether *Jane Eyre* or *Wuthering Heights* was the better novel but agreed on Anne's work and made it our goal to read *Agnes Grey* each year.

We discovered Janette Oke together and committed to reading every book she put out. Her marriage of faith with romance blossoming in pioneer settings must have been written for us.

Bellum's librarian appreciated our regular business and held our favorites as soon as they arrived. New book day became our personal holiday.

Long before I met Carolina and first experienced the joy of true friendship, I found comfort and kinship between the covers of books. They drew me away from the emptiness of my childhood dwelling into a realm where homes—not just lifeless houses—existed.

Stories gave my heart love and life to strive for when I had neither.

The bright spot of my childhood in California was the location of our house. One block down and half a block back stood a building that looked like a castle. The architecture nodded to earlier times and faraway places.

I'm not sure how many times, awestruck and overwhelmed, I stood in front of the entrance before I tucked my hands into determined fists and scaled the great stairs. All my strength barely cracked the door wide enough to squeeze inside.

At eight years old, I watched my world instantly broaden as my eyes adjusted to the dim setting of endless rows of the brightest objects I'd ever seen—books. More books than I thought existed in the world, let alone in one building so near to my lonely house.

"May I help you find what you're looking for?"

She was a librarian, no doubt—bun, glasses on a chain, cardigan. Beneath twinkling hazel eyes, shone the kindest smile I'd ever received.

My initial warmth at her glow chilled, and I dropped my chin. "Oh ... I don't have any money."

Her laugh reminded me of a music box one of mom's friends had given me for my fifth birthday.

"You don't need money here, sweetie. All you need is a library card. Would you like one of those?"

My eyes must have reflected the confusion I was unraveling because the woman continued, "With a library card, you can check out any book you want for free. You get to take it home with you for four weeks. Bring it back and check out a new one. I can give you the application for your mother to fill out and then we can get your card all ready for you."

My heart felt like it had been traveling up and down the wavy mountains in a Mickey Mouse cartoon, but this drop jolted me hardest. "Oh. My mother isn't with me today."

This time, I saw a look in her eyes I often saw in my teachers'—I was too young then to recognize pity and concern. She recovered quickly and held out her hand. "That's okay; I can send the papers with you. You just bring them back once she's had a chance to fill them out, and I'll fix your card up myself. Until then, though, I think it would be okay for you to pick out a book or two. You may use my card. Will you bring them back in four weeks?"

I felt the sparkle in my eyes as I nodded and swore an unspoken promise to care for the books and return them sooner than she asked.

She helped me choose two books: *Thumbelina* and *Charlotte's Web*. I carried them and the papers she had given me with all the care of a mother with a just-born infant. As I escaped into the worlds within the books' pages, I found the wooden paneling of our den no longer dreary and the bright pink and purple décor of my room less garish. Food had more flavor. The sun shone brighter, and I wasn't quite so lonely anymore.

Storytellers and their characters had entered my life and revealed portals to new realms I'd never dared to imagine.

Not quite a week later, I returned to the magical castle of books with my mother who was finally awake during their business hours. My librarian friend didn't look sideways at the lack of length to my mother's skirt or the excessive height of her heels. She welcomed her with the same genuine smile I remembered.

Mom must have been enamored with the beauty of the building and kindness of its keeper as well because we both exited with cards and books. Further, I carried away a dream to one day work with books in a library or bookstore and share stories of joy with lonely children like me.

With each visit, I chose more books by Hans Christian Anderson and E.B. White and rapidly advanced to Laura Ingalls Wilder's pioneering series where I couldn't get enough of the beauty that was Pa and Ma.

A father and mother—together—with their children. A man who stuck around, built houses, grew food and protected his family. A woman who cooked and baked everything from scratch, who sewed clothes and mended wounds. A couple who personified toughness and tenderness in perfect harmony.

The stories I gravitated toward instilled a second dream—one for a solid family and sure future with them. I could be saved from my lonely life where my parent was a woman who pursued her princes at wild parties. To her credit, my mother gave me an example of the life I never wanted.

Less than a decade later, when Jack strolled into the diner where I served tables, I believed my prince had come. He talked about far-off places: Santa Fe, Colorado Springs, Washington State. He always closed his tales with, "There's somethin' bout that Georgia clay."

On my graduation day, he asked for my hand. With no one to speak for me, I said yes, cleared my few possessions from the rented house that had never been a home and sent a message to my mom through all of her crowd I could find.

Whether or not she got the message, I don't know. Reports from her acquaintances varied from "Last saw her in the county morgue" to "She's gone out east" to "She hit it big with some businessman with a fat wallet."

Nothing held me back, so off we went. We zigzagged across the country, visiting places I'd only seen in books. Jack took me all the way to Niagara Falls. Under the spritz of the water and the tease of the wind, I told him I wanted to settle down, have babies, make a home … somewhere pretty, somewhere safe, somewhere sure.

Somewhere outside his wandering nature.

The spell of the falls must have been strong because his eyes took on an unusual shimmer and his smile filled his face.

Over the roar of the crashing falls, he yelled, "I know just the place. There's somethin' bout that Georgia clay."

Driving along the backwoods highways of northeast Georgia, Jack stopped and reversed our battered camper truck to park alongside a sign: "Bellum, population 4,898."

"Doesn't that sound homey? That's the place for us, Becky. Think you can call Bellum home?"

"With you, I can."

We coasted into our new hometown on fumes and fabricated dreams. Jack found a job at a sawmill thirty minutes away just before we opened our final can of pork and beans. After a while of living in our tiny camper, we saved enough for a lease-to-own on an old house that looked like a mansion to us. We had a place of our own, and my dream of family seemed to be coming true. At the time, that was all the happily ever after I needed.

His eyes first signaled me in that greasy diner. They beckoned, much like a lighthouse flashes home's safety to ships at sea. Back then, I thought of myself as the ship.

How our roles flipped.

Forever never featured in his future. What drew me to his gold-speckled irises wasn't their color or shape. Certainly not the way he looked at me, though I interpreted his gazes as I longed them to be. Fairy tales and *Happily Ever Afters* fueled my overactive imagination and tricked the light into casting us as a starring family. What hypnotized me beneath his long lashes was wanderlust that manifested to me as fearlessness.

That feigned attribute cast his spell over me when I was young and lonely. I wanted a man as brave and true and committed as Pa, and so I projected those desired traits onto him. The trouble is, like water and oil, reality and my imagination didn't mix.

Jack started coming home late a couple nights a week. I didn't mind much. A man needs a night out for a few drinks with his buddies, right?

A couple turned to most nights, and I wondered if that was how married life worked. I'd never observed a marriage or even the home life of a man. All I knew came from movies and shows—men needed attention, a clean home and hot meals. Movies never showed men bringing much back to women, other than the occasional slain dragon.

That was about the time my fairy tale ran past midnight and the carriage and stallions reverted to a pumpkin and mice. The look in Jack's eyes that I'd initially loved resurfaced. The difference was I now understood it had nothing to do with fearlessness and everything to do with discontent and an innate need to roam.

When he disappeared, he left a two-word note:

I'm sorry.

He also credited to me his debts and a realization that I had no idea who I was outside of him. I was twenty-four with no education past high school and no career goals, aside from my distant childhood dream to be a kind librarian or bookshop owner.

My reality was I had a child to care for in a tiny town that didn't put much emphasis on literature.

What I knew how to do was work hard, survive and disappear into fairy tales. The only catch was my old favorite stories no longer warmed my heart. Each one became a taunting example of yet another thing I wouldn't have—happy endings meant for anyone but me.

Life didn't stop for goodbyes or wishes on stars. Time carried on, and so did I. Dreams became antique notions that belonged tucked away in mothball-filled chests.

Then a realization struck, *Dreams never belonged to me.*

Like a will-o'-the-wisp, what I thought I had grasped slipped through my fingers and drifted away into the dark woods that my future now resembled. I only thought my dreams had come true. The past six years were merely fantasy fiction ... except for the golden-eyed boy who relied on me to care for him. He was real and my greatest gift.

I grieved for a time but adjusted to the lifestyle of a single working parent. Once little Jack and I settled into a routine, Carolina reminded me of my love for stories. We read together again. Our book club reignited my love of stories and soothed my soul with the healing power of words.

Carolina was the one who exposed my belief that dreams lay outside my grasp as a lie. Of course, it's taken me more than twenty years to act on her wisdom. I suppose my son gets his stubborn nature as much from me as from his father.

On club nights, I'd bring the brownies, and Carolina would pull our lamp off the top shelf in her coat closet. With small children running around, we didn't dare leave it out every day. I made Carolina store it because I figured Jack would find a way to break it or spill the oil, even tucked in a high place behind a closed door. Boys are clever like that.

During that season, Carolina taught me how to study the Bible. I discovered more about God's nature—His holiness, love, kindness and sacrifice. I learned more about myself—a sinner, saved by grace and covered in Christ's righteousness.

Jesus' parables of the lost coin and the lost sheep spoke directly to me. I felt forgotten, like a sheep—alone and far from the safe grassy meadow, perilously close to tumbling off a precipice in the fog of loneliness.

Reading Jesus' words and discussing them with Carolina showed me how wrong I was. My God will not cast me away. Instead, He will catch and cradle me like the helpless lamb I am.

In fiction books, we witnessed the beauty of everyday faith lived out in women throughout history—the pastor's wife in Victorian England who showed kindness to all classes of people, the mother on the prairie determined to keep the homestead running during her husband's extended recovery from a tragic accident, the young schoolteacher terrified of failing in the mountain school where books came second to survival.

With each happily ever after we reached, I grew more gloomy. One evening, Carolina turned toward my dramatic sigh.

I complained, "Maybe we need to read a tragedy. These happily ever afters are getting to me. Dreams never belonged to me the way they do to these women."

Our lamp flickered across her face. I'll never forget how, in each cast of its brightness, another emotion emerged: surprise in the slight lift of her eyebrow, sorrow in the mist rising in her eyes, empathy in the tilt of her face, love and conviction in the words she spoke.

"Just because horrible events and disappointing people have filled your life to this point does not mean you cannot dream."

Carolina reached out to me, and we held hands in front of our club lamp.

She continued, "What you said about dreams not belonging to you is a lie that breeds discontent and despair. Satan wants you to believe it's true because he is the king of despair. Your past does not dictate your future, especially with God lighting your pathway forward. Cling to His light as you remember He created you. He made you to bring Him honor and glory, and He planned for you to do that by living out your dreams for Him."

Tears freely flowed down my cheeks as Carolina talked. Her words convicted and altered me. Through her influence, I cut the ties that bound me to that soul-crushing lie. She showed me that God held my future in His hands, and I had no reason to doubt He included good things in my tomorrows.

Though I still couldn't see how this truth applied to my specific dream of working in a bookstore, I felt peace in the future for the first time. Though I may not have the family I envisioned, my son was a more special gift than dreams could have shown me. Family takes on more than one framework, and I recognized that dream still alive and well in my life.

Peace remained with me through the valleys of Carolina's cancer treatments and the shadow of her death.

I grieved harder than ever. My best friend on this earth was gone. I felt her loss intrinsically and wondered how I could move forward.

Through all my grief, though, God held me like the lamb to which He likens me. I felt His comfort and His presence. For the first time, I understood what my friend had always told me about God never leaving us or forsaking us because I knew He was with me. Even without Carolina's presence, I'll never be alone because God will always be with me.

My dream of family remains fulfilled. Jack and Rachael grew up and, despite life's best attempts, never grew out of love for each other. After their wedding, they'll live in the second apartment above this shop that Jack and I share. Ben lives nearby, and we have family dinners together at least once a week. Carolina's memory and love infuse our lives and unite us.

Beyond all that ... though God's gift of family and home could be enough ... I still have books.

Stories possess a magic unique to the written word. Whether a book was written thousands of years ago or yesterday, by someone like me or someone I have nothing in common with, stories allow me to experience other lives, to form a bond with people I'll never meet and to learn who I am and who I can be.

Books, like Carolina, remind me dreams do belong to me.

And so, a year-and-a-half ago, when my son returned to me, God had been preparing my heart through the books I read.

The Guernsey Literary and Potato Peel Pie Society filled me with courage to follow my dreams, no matter how silly others would think them. *The Bookshop* hit a bit more on the nose with the widow who took the impractical leap and opened a bookstore.

When Jack reentered life and reestablished our family after his prodigal years, he shared with me his dreams to open a shop to sell his furniture and other handmade items.

The fire in his voice and light in his eyes reminded me of our book club lamp. So, when he asked about my dreams, I spoke my one unfulfilled dream out loud for the first time since before Carolina's death.

"I have always wanted to work in a bookshop. You know—the kind with kiddie chairs for story hour. Where I can help others find stories that will inspire and entertain and enlighten them ... books that will encourage them to dream."

My son took my hand and said, "That makes perfect sense, but why just work in a bookshop? Why not own one?"

The old belief—as big a lie as ever—popped back in my head along with a host of excuses:

I don't have enough money

How could I do something like that by myself?

I'm too old.

Where would I open it?

Jack overturned each doubt until the only thought left standing in my mind was the dream that had hidden in my heart for so long.

Today, that dream came true, complete with a giant ribbon and pair of scissors and a street full of supportive book lovers, eager to peruse the shelves I smile at now.

I open my arms to embrace the air around me as I turn a lazy circle inside my new shop. Nearly a half century on this earth, and I have finally embraced this dream.

Carolina's joy from that antique shopping trip long ago washes over me again. I see a glint from the lamp in the fresh tear looming in the corner of my eye.

"I did listen, Carolina, though it took me a while to act. Over the years, my dream of family has finally morphed into this collaboration of our two families. Remembering your words and clinging to God's promises, I walked hand in hand with Jack to embrace this second dream. Thank you for your gift of friendship and belief in my dreams."

Around me, books cast their rainbow of dreams and memories in the illumination of our lamp.

War & Peaches

Romantic notions have no place in wartime.

That bein' said, love stubbornly blooms amid bombs and bloodshed, and war's horrors don't always shatter the soul.

Between the years 1942 and 1946, I matured as I don't rightly think I would have without the war. My part in it felt big at the time; my Pat's part was far bigger than I knew. Even the German prisoners' part impacted us in ways we never could've imagined.

To best understand my story, you ought to know who I was and where I came from. I'm sorry to admit, I was a spoiled priss. When mama died soon after I was born, Daddy took all the doting he'd always given her and heaped it on me—times a hundred. He'd whisper in my ear as he rocked me to sleep, "My sweet Mabel girl, you'll never want for a pretty thing as long as I'm your daddy."

As the youngest of ten, the only girl and Daddy's little princess, I didn't worry about much more than the dress I would wear to the next social event. I had a fair few of those to look forward to. Daddy'd sit down with me at the beginnin' of each season and make a fuss over my social calendar.

He'd fret about if I'd have enough dresses and always asked my favorite color. Course he didn't really need to ask; emerald green brought out my eyes and popped against my creamy skin and dark hair. He'd take his time, jotting down every detail I flung his way—fabrics, new techniques and all the latest embellishments. Our local seamstress loved to see my daddy walkin' in twice a year with his big ol' list.

Daddy was a farmer—the best in Aiken County and, probably, South Carolina. He had what he called "an abundance of land." That sayin' usually paired with his booming laugh that reminded me of a marchin' band in parades and picnics on the town square.

Mamie was our housekeeper and cook. She'd lived with us ever since her husband and son died in the flu outbreak before I was born. I had a nurse and, when I got older, a tutor. They all served as mother figures of a sort as I grew. A few of my sisters-in-law filled that role as well. I was the youngest by a good number of years, after all.

My brothers—the seven still with us—teased as older brothers do, but they also protected. Few fellas were brave enough to call on me, guarded as I was. As I got older, though, Daddy began inviting young men to dinner. He'd inquire about their businesses in Charleston and Savannah or about their families. After months of uncomfortable dinners where the young men asked the most inane questions about my education and preferences for dance styles at an upcoming ball, Daddy called me into his study.

"Mabel, darling, it seems to me you're not keen on any of the upstanding young fellas I've been bringing around to make your acquaintance."

"Oh, Daddy! Is that what all these silly dinners have been about?"

I couldn't imagine why on earth he thought I'd be interested in any of those stuffy old suits.

"Why, yes, my dear girl! It's my task as your father to ensure you make a proper match with a man who can keep you in the comfort you deserve in a house worthy of a lady of your caliber."

"Pshaw!" I rounded his desk and lowered to my knees, green skirts encircling me. "Daddy, all I want is to live right here on this land I know as home. I love this house and the animals and the rows without end of fresh vegetables and our stately peach orchard. I love you and my brothers. I love their families and every one of their homesteads dotted around us. I don't need some fancy-talkin' man in a suitcoat with his slicked-back hair talkin' bout how much his beef cattle could fetch at market."

Daddy leaned down, a twinkle in his eye, and said, "Think of how many fine dresses those cattle could buy you."

Our laughter duet filled the room as he pulled me to my feet. The twinkle in his eyes took on a sheen as he said, "I just want a good man for you, my sweet Mabel girl."

"When the right one comes along, I reckon I'll figure it out before you will, don't you think?"

I was an impertinent little miss. Daddy shook his head, grinned and sprouted a worry line or two. Lookin' back, I know he wanted me to be properly cared for if anything were to happen to him. He wasn't exactly a spring chicken.

§

During plantin' and harvest, Daddy hired extra laborers. They'd stick around a few weeks and then be off again to wherever driftin' workers went. Every now and then, though, one stood out as a hard worker and stayed on as a permanent part of Daddy's team.

He called them "his team" on account of not one of us is in this world alone and not one of us can do everything by ourselves, a truth he took every chance to remind us. He expected us all to work hard—well, I reckon he meant that part more for my brothers than me—and to work with others.

"We're all better together," he'd say.

I think Daddy's conviction came from his experience as an orphan in a strange country. He was born in Ireland, and his Ulster-Irish parents moved him to the U.S. when he was ten. Before his twelfth birthday, they died, and he found himself at the mercy of strangers. A successful and generous farmer became his benefactor and taught Daddy all he knew.

The green of Ireland must've infused his thumb, 'cause Daddy took to farmin' like a duck to water. He improved and expanded all the crops so much that they bought more land. He inherited every lick of that land when the older farmer died, and it was the only home I'd ever known.

Back to the workers daddy hired: one of them was Patrick Miller. He was nineteen that harvest of '39 and what a looker—with his expressive blue eyes and thick hair.

I was seventeen and had set my father straight about the potential suitors he'd been bringing around. My mind wasn't on marrying yet. I had no desire to take charge of a household or move away from a place where my every need was met in full, but Pat caught my eye the first time I saw him. So much so, I found reasons to happen around wherever he was working.

It wasn't until the following summer—June 1940, to be exact—that we finally spoke. He never did more than tuck his head and tip his hat when he passed me. Some men tended to be on the shy side—on account of my daddy's and brothers' eagle eyes—so I figured he needed a nudge.

One afternoon, I saw him out in the orchard alone and moseyed along in his direction. Pat sized up every hanging fruit before pickin', all while I kept up a procession of chatter about the weather, the peaches, upcoming social gatherings and the new dresses I expected to receive later that week. He'd nod on occasion and tip his head at me whenever he moved his baskets to the next tree. Not a single word, though … until I twirled to leave.

After my forty-five-minute soliloquy, I decided he was downright rude, and I'd take my leave and never again give him the time of day. I do believe I even *humphed* as I bid him a curt "Good day, Mr. Miller" and turned on my heels.

"Miss Mabel, you might like these here peaches."

The first sentence I'd ever heard from Pat's mouth made me drop my chin and swallow a gnat. Apology and hope twinkled in his eyes as he offered the fruit to me. He had to know how fond I was of our peaches.

He handed me the two best specimens of the bushels he'd been picking, and I handed him my heart.

I lowered myself to the ground, spread my skirt and handed a peach back to him. When I patted the grass beside me, he obliged and sat, one leg bent with his arm propped on that knee. We reveled in the glory that is a fresh peach and giggled like schoolchildren as juice trickled down our arms. He told me about his home and family hardware store in Columbia.

"Hardy's has been in the family a few generations now. No idea why the name—no Hardys in our lineage."

"Why are you workin' for my daddy? It's hot as anything out here and your back's gotta be aching. Wouldn't you rather be workin' in a store where the sun won't beat down on you?"

He polished off the rest of his peach and examined the rough, ragged pit. Though he didn't use near as many words as I did, Pat spoke deep thoughts.

"Sweat and a sore back mean ya' put in a good day's work." He sucked the remaining juice off the pit as he stood. "Somethin' satisfyin' bout that."

By the time Pat helped me to my feet, I knew I'd found the man for me. I marched straight to Daddy's office and informed him of my choice. He wasn't too pleased with the prospect, though I knew he admired Pat's work ethic. I'd overheard him tell my brothers Pat was the hardest worker they'd ever had.

Daddy determined I needed a man with more means to keep me in the comfort I'd grown up knowin'. He launched a new dinner guest campaign until I stood up in the middle of a meal, tossed my napkin on my heaping plate and stormed out of the dinin' room. A minute later Daddy found me, pacing in his study. I felt the flush on my cheeks.

"Did you really think I'd keep sittin' there after he went on and on about 'the dirty workers' you landowners must employ these days and your 'unnecessary evil to pay folks who should've been content with their place?' Oh, Daddy! I don't ever want to see that vile man again, and I would like to have Pat join us for dinner. I know you like him as a worker, and he makes me happy. Won't you give him a chance?"

Daddy crossed the floor and wrapped me in his strong embrace. "My sweet Mabel girl, I want for you all the very best of everything you could possibly have in this life."

"What if all the very best I desire is the love and devotion of a man who works harder than any of your other workers and who genuinely cares about me?"

His response rumbled against the ear I pressed to his chest. "I'd say you desire something right and good indeed."

With a gentle kiss on my forehead, Daddy walked to the door. "I'll handle our current guest—not my wisest choice, I agree—and perhaps you'd like to write an invitation to your chosen suitor for tomorrow's dinner."

An unladylike squeal and dash up the stairs revealed an overflowin' heart. I restrained myself from running out to the workers' cabins since that would be too indecorous, even for me.

§

With my father's blessin' over us, me and Pat were thicker than Mamie's pea soup straight out of the refrigerator. He asked me to wait for his hand until he'd saved enough for his own farm. He didn't want to live off the land my father had cultivated; he wanted to make his own way. I understood his heart, and my father respected his ambition.

While Pat worked, I'd ramble on and on about our wedding and my dress and the flowers and the food and how many guests we'd have. He'd smile and nod every now and then. Whenever he looked my way, though, the sparkle in his blue eyes told me he loved me as much as I loved him; he just didn't need as many words as I did to express it. We planned to marry after the harvest in 1942, and I declared peach cider should replace the typical wedding punch. Our plans were set, and our dreams were big.

December 7, 1941, changed them all.

Pat joined us at the house that next day to listen to President Roosevelt rally our nation in response to the attacks on Pearl Harbor. And then, we were at war—not just any war, another world-wide war.

Those aboard the ships that faced the onslaught of Japan's bombs were our brothers and friends and beaus. They were the lifeblood of our nation, and we would see their deaths avenged.

While spirits soared and patriotism was the accessory of the day, I couldn't feel anything but numbness. The Great War still haunted the minds of many. I saw its effects daily in the shadows of my oldest brother's eyes, in my second oldest brother's limp and in the absence of my brother James, whose zest for life and dreams to be an explorer greater than Lewis or Clark I knew only from stories. He never got to chase those dreams, and the War that took him from us should have kept such horror from happening again.

And yet, it didn't.

I knew Pat would join. He didn't have to tell me. He did ask, "Would you be willing to move up our wedding?"

The ceremony was small; my dress simple. Daddy wept through his smile as he placed my hand in Pat's. We said our *I do*s with the call to arms echoing around us. Our family hosted a small reception afterward, and Mamie fulfilled my desire for peach cider. Our time as husband and wife was sweet, but short. We savored that Christmas together, mindful it could be our only.

Pat enlisted with the Marine Corps. He said, "Anything worth doin's worth doin' at its best."

The night before he headed to Parris Island for a shortened four-week Boot Camp, I was as big a mess as biscuit dough with too much buttermilk.

"Maybe you don't really have to go. They've got lots of others to fight. They won't miss just you. Can't you tell them you changed your mind? I know! The Old Testament talks about Israelite men not going off to war for a year after they married. Tell them you just married! Oh, Pat! We just said our 'til death do us parts, and I don't want you to die! Please don't die. You can't; you just can't! What would I do without you? How will I be able to stand it, sittin' here waitin' on you to come on home? You will come home, though, you will; and I'll be waitin'. I won't just be sittin', though. No siree! Your favorite's buttermilk biscuits, and I'm gonna learn to make them. You'll see! I'll learn to make sawmill gravy, too. You better come on home quick, so I can fatten you up with my new cookin' skills. I'll make you homemade peach cobbler, too— with only the freshest and best of our peaches. I'll pick 'em like you do."

"Breathe, dear," Pat interjected. "I believe you'll do ev'ry bit of that and more. I'll come home to you; I promise."

The bus carried him to training, and my heart went with him—along with my health. I woke up sick every morning and could barely hold down food. Sleepin' didn't come easy either. Wide eyes in the middle of the night saw only terror. I lay there frettin' about the *what if*s until my stomach flipped on me and I stumbled toward the commode.

My mind convinced me that my ailing stemmed from saying goodbye to my new husband. After a few weeks, Daddy smiled as he replaced the cold rag on my forehead and asked, "Mabel, dear, have you considered you might be with child?"

I sputtered like an old pickup on a ragged dirt road while the idea bounced around my mind. Daddy'd already left my room when I placed a hand on my belly and declared, "Oh my!"

§

Pat received a brief leave after training. Wouldn't you know, he'd impressed somebody and got himself picked up for a brand-new unit. Chest puffed out, he greeted me with a kiss and a spinning hug that nearly sent me searchin' for a ladies' room.

"The Marines are formin' a new battalion, and I'll be part of it. I'll be a Marine Raider, Mabel! We'll start out probably up in Quantico, but then ..."

"I'm expectin'!"

I clapped a hand over my mouth, shocked at how I'd blurted our news to him—but more so at interrupting him talkin' more than I'd ever heard in one sitting.

Emotions shifted across his eyes, and I watched them grow real soft, yet solid ... like a poached egg. I saw his surprise, concern, pride—a glimmer of fear—but mostly love. He took my hands in his and drew me to him, gently. His love and surety cascaded over me as he wrapped me in his arms, and I sank into my home. We remained interlocked quite a while—people bustling around us as we held on for our lives.

We didn't have much time. That didn't keep us from packin' years' worth of togetherness into it, though. We talked about our future and our baby. Pat told me all the things he'd teach our son. I couldn't convince him we might have a girl.

"Nah! That's my boy in there; I guarantee it."

He'd wink and smile and silence my ramblin' rebuttals with a kiss. I faked annoyance with him, but I could never stay angry at my Pat. He had this way of smoothing over any fightin' words he'd toss out—like foldin' fresh cream into pudding. We'd mix together, velvety as you please, even when disagreeing.

It seemed I hadn't taken a full breath before he shipped out again. This goodbye stood differently, more finality around its edges—like a tough crust on day-old homemade bread that sat uncovered.

We knew where he was going and what could prevent his return. Despite his Raider bravado and declaration that he'd be back in time for me to have his son, we knew the reality. I waved a handkerchief at the bus that carried my Pat away from me. My future flew away with the motion, swirling in the dust cloud of that fast-moving thief.

§

While Pat continued training for war, we received sugar ration coupons. Seems fitting, the first thing to go in wartime is the sweetness.

Since we lived on a farm, we didn't feel too put out with the rationing. Daddy had increased his crop plantin' for the government. They had millions of troops to feed, and our farm helped a small percentage. Mamie and I planted a victory garden for most of our table's food.

I chose my Pat's favorites since I figured our baby might share his hankerings. We had beans and peas; rows of big, juicy tomatoes; carrots and lettuce. The squash featured in another of Pat's favorite dishes—squash casserole. Of course, we didn't have as much butter as usual. Food without the proper amount of butter doesn't quite measure up to our high Southern standards, but we made do.

Mamie played a vital role in our enjoyment of sweets. One summer afternoon in 1942—around the time Pat was on a ship leavin' the United States—I tied an apron around my rapidly expandin' middle in preparation for another cooking lesson. Mamie led me to our home's food storage and a mound covered with burlap sacks. She sighed before talkin'.

"I hope you won't think bad of me. Durin' the War, we didn't have no sugar, couldn't get it anywheres. So's we went all them years without a proper cobbler. When the fightin' started over with the Germans this time round, I started buyin' an extra sack here and there and tuckin' them away. Just in case."

She lifted the sacks to reveal a stockpile that would last us all the way until 1947 when sugar rationing finally ended. I stared, wide-eyed, back and forth between her sheepish face and the pile of sugary goodness. When I doubled over in a laughing fit, Mamie joined me, halting at first—a sputtered chuckle here, then there. Finally, we clutched one another to remain upright as we allowed the absurd humor of the situation to remove any shame we might have felt.

The Great Wall of Sugar, as we called it, remained our secret throughout the war. The men thanked us for our delicious cooking and complimented the treats we coaxed from our few "tasty rations," as they called them. We'd share a giggle and answer with a simple, "Oh, you're most welcome!" or "Why, thank you!"

§

Letters from Pat arrived slowly and sporadically, but we kept sentiments traveling across the land and sea between us. He couldn't write details of where they were or what they were doing. I kept my notes light and airy, like the biscuits I was learning to make.

In one of his early letters, Pat shared some of his experiences during their travels. Neither of us had ventured much past the South Carolina border, let alone beyond the opposite ocean.

Dearest Mabel,

We live in a mighty impressive nation! I've seen mountains and prairies and forests with trees you wouldn't believe—I'm still not sure they have tops. I never saw them. The Pacific Ocean is blue and green and overwhelming. I'm beginning to wonder if our earth is really round and if we'll ever reach our destination.

In another letter, he wrote about the beauty in the islands where they were.

Dearest Mabel,

I won't always be able to tell you where we are, but I think it's safe to write that we've arrived in Samoa. These islands are covered with American military uniforms right now. All of us coming over to give the Japs the what-for stop here first.

Remember how I wrote about the blue-green of the Pacific Ocean? The water here is clear as crystals—I can see to the bottom! All the fish swimming around down there without a clue of the war up here come in every color of the rainbow, and then some.

These islands are something else, too. They look like giant bobbing bushes from a distance. They're volcanic islands, and the green comes from the rainforests ... can you believe that?

The people here are some of the smilingest folks you'll ever see. I think you'd like it here. Maybe one day we can return for the honeymoon we missed.

We never did take that vacation. I don't think Pat was keen on returning to those islands.

§

That summer of '42 got hotter and hotter while I got fatter and fatter. Mamie helped me put my sewin' skills and overflowing closet of well-made dresses to proper war use. We repurposed several for the remainder of my maternity time and tucked a few away to be mended and simplified for future use.

Most of my wardrobe went to the young girls of Aiken County. They needn't miss out on style if I could help it. Others, we set aside to make rompers for my little one.

The baby made sure I knew he was in there—I called our little one a him, too, but I still teased Pat in my letters about us having a girl. The baby's kicks kept me from sleeping or restin' or finding any comfortable position. About the only time he didn't kick was when I bustled round the kitchen with Mamie.

She had the patience of Job with me. After a few times of me burnin' butter and other rations it was a sin to waste, Mamie kept a closer eye on me. She explained how things smell just before they're ready for the next step. Thanks to my carelessness, I experienced a few of the smells that come a second past, too.

§

Summer continued into September with no hint of autumn's breezes. My time was comin'.

Dearest Mabel,

I'm not sure when I'll write again. We sail for another island tomorrow. I don't expect to have much leisure time once we land. I love you, and I love our son. No more nonsense about us having a daughter. You'll see.

The day after I received his letter, I did see.

Pat Junior was born on September 23, 1942, while—thousands of miles away—his father recovered from one of the biggest battles he'd fought yet. I prayed through every pain of birth for my son's healthy delivery and for my husband's safety and quick return to meet his namesake.

Pat's letter had taken nearly a month to reach me. I couldn't know that, since he wrote that letter, Pat had been one of Edson's Raiders in the Battle of Bloody Ridge. The title was enough to give me nightmares.

His next letter arrived a few days before November. Thankfully he received my news of our son's arrival before they shipped away from Guadalcanal for a needed rest.

Dearest Mabel,

I told you we were having a boy! I'm so proud of you and him! We don't have much in the way of cigars on hand, but the boys have each given me a couple of cigarettes from their rations. I promise not to pick up a foul habit, but I think a little celebration wouldn't be too wrong in this case.

We're finally leaving our first big battle. The island's in U.S. hands now—no easy task. We lost many great men.

I got a bit of a cut on my leg that will likely leave a scar. Promise not to fuss over it too much when I get home. Word is we're due some R&R. Not sure how long, though. I wish I could be there with you and our son.

I love you. Kiss him for me.

Thankfully, I didn't know at the time how deep that cut had been. I didn't know how bloody the battle had been or that it wouldn't be the worst he'd see. I know now it was a miracle, though he never shared all the details of what he survived.

He told me when he came home that the nightmares were for him to carry—like he'd carried arms—so I can live in the peace of a world removed from war. His actions hid in his nightmares until he could speak them to a group of fellow fighters at the American Legion.

§

Though I missed my husband somethin' awful, especially during those hazy first months of our son's life, I had plenty of help from Mamie, my sisters-in-law and brothers.

Daddy was a perfect Grandpappy to little Pat. He helped with burpin' and even diaper changes. As time passed and little Pat grew, they became best buddies.

I'd usually find Daddy bouncin' him on his knee in a rocker on our front porch. Once my son took to toddling about, Daddy'd lead him by the hand, showin' him what plants were what and teachin' him how to pick peaches and eat them straight away.

The white-haired man and the wide-eyed tyke taking the world in with the curiosity of a spindly-legged calf made quite the pair as they ambled hand in hand through the orchard or sat on the porch. Daddy discussed crops and birds and whatever else came to mind with his grandson.

When little Pat spent time with me, I was usually elbow-deep in flour (when we had it) or in potato peels (which we usually had). He'd help Mamie and me in the kitchen, while I'd tell him tales of his Pop.

By help, I mean he sat near us with a snack or played at our feet with wooden blocks. And, by tales, I mean I'd talk about his Pop's favorite foods and how good he was at picking the right peaches at the perfect time. I told little Pat how his Pop was bein' a brave Marine and keepin' us safe.

Though I kept talk of killin' and my feelings for our faraway enemies out of my stories to my year-and-a-half-old son, I corralled anger in my heart and fed it a generous diet of hate.

We received word that my brother Nicholas—the one closest to me in age and friendship—had been taken prisoner by the Germans. Thinkin' of him locked away in a land of atrocities too awful to believe shocked me to my core. Letters from my other brother Charles, who fought somewhere in Europe, and from my Pat arrived too slowly.

The more the war seeped into our home through headlines and radio and the longer my Pat was separated from me, the darker my heart grew. Every day was another twenty-four hours of Japanese bullets and grenades raining down on him and 1,440 minutes closer to him not making it home.

Each season deepened my loathing for the people who upended my world, stole my comforts and left me alone with a son who'd never met his father. Letting my hatred fester did nothin' but make me bitter and far from Christian in thought.

Daddy noticed it consumin' me and led me out for a "turn around the land," as he called it. We strolled in peaceful silence.

I sniffed and wondered why flowers always smell sweetest in April. I wished my Pat could enjoy them with me. He'd been gone more than two years, and I wondered—as I often did—how he was and where he was.

We reached a freshly tilled field. As I gazed across the fluffy mounds of earth, I inhaled their damp richness and pondered the promise for new life they contained. Daddy's words sliced through my thoughts.

"When I was not much older than little Pat, I knew hatred. It often centered across the pages of the Bible back in Ulster; Catholics and Protestants at odds often came to blows. Being raised with that roiling around me, I was a temperamental youth. Anger seeped into my actions toward my fellow man. Losing my parents soon after moving here didn't make me less ireful. I was a twelve-year-old orphan in a strange place without a friend in the world. Or so I thought."

Daddy's chuckle and wink lightened his tone as he guided me to sit on a fallen tree before perchin' beside me.

"You know how the Sanders took me in. They showed me a kindness I hadn't expected. More than that, they lived out love and compassion for all humanity. In a place filled with hate toward folks who might be a different shade and toward those who didn't uphold the 'value' of hatin' them, Farmer Sanders and his wife gave me an example of a better way to live.

Hearing the gospel at First Presbyterian every Sunday and watching it lived out all week changed my outlook on life and on my fellow man. It squeezed out the anger and hate—like pus from a festering wound."

When Daddy used such crass language—as he would call it—I knew his message was important. What he'd been sayin' had already begun to release the foul emotions I'd kept bottled within me. I felt them bubbling over the walls of my heart, tingling on their paths toward escape.

"Without that infection inside, I was a changed person— one who saw others as my fellow travelers on this earth, companions for the journey. When we entered the Great War and your three oldest brothers joined, I had an important job: produce good food and care for those left behind until our men returned. Hating the other side wouldn't help me accomplish my tasks."

I studied my hands and the simple gold band I wore. I fingered the locket around my neck and envisioned the photographs inside—Pat and me at our wedding and little Pat. My tasks were caring for our son and helping Mamie with the house. I wrapped my hand around the locket, stinging from the pang of a realization that my loathing could infect my child.

"When your two brothers returned and we buried the third without his body, I faced a new round of anger and hate."

I watched mist spread across Daddy's expression. In the hardening of his jaw and the ache pulsin' from his skin, I sensed the pain he'd endured over the years. Daddy's parents' accident. My mother's death. The loss of James in the War and then Thomas who was only four when the flu hit. With so much grief and loss in his life, how could Daddy exude kindness and joy?

"For a while, I didn't know how to beat the hate. We had nearly lost George, too. William Jr. might have looked fine, but his wounds ran deep. He wouldn't talk about those trenches."

Daddy rubbed his hands along his thighs and straightened on our makeshift bench. He surprised me with a chuckle.

"Chopping wood became my outlet, which meant we had more fuel than we'd need for three winters. One afternoon William joined me in the midst of my axe-slinging and talked. The things he told me, I won't repeat. The point is, that talk was the start of his healing—and mine. He taught me that war wounds the soul. I already knew rage becomes a fast-spreading cancer in our souls. One of those is bad enough; combine the two, and they're often deadly. Both can be treated, but it takes time and communication. And love."

Daddy looked directly at me and continued. "William had to start talking, but Lillian's love was the medicine that stopped the spread of the disease in his heart. His return to church with his wife and us smoothed some of the scars. Watching him heal and begin to forgive and live again reminded me of a most important truth. Goodness, light and love come from One Source, and that's where I had to turn for my own heart change and soul healing."

As Daddy's hands, roughened by work-carved caverns, enshrined my own, he concluded his heart revelation to me. "Watching Charles and Nicholas—and your Patrick—march off to this war reminded me of those lessons. My prayer has been that I wouldn't allow hate to control me again. I've also prayed that their soul wounds won't rend them in two or separate them from truth and mercy. To help them, though, we must keep sight of the light and strengthen our love now so we can cover them when they return. Our task means not just letting go of the anger toward our enemies; it means learning to love them."

Daddy's words seeped into my heart. The call to not hate wasn't enough. Beyond that must come forgiveness and even love. Could I accept my wartime orders? Could I follow them?

Pat was off fightin'—not just because of duty, though. He told me on our last night together that he signed up for pride and vengeance, but we—me and little Pat—were his reason to fight, to follow the orders, to fulfill his mission. Presented with my own charge, I realized he and our son were my reasons.

"You're right, of course, Daddy."

My voice drifted small to my ears as I felt the weight of all I'd held pressin' on my insides—like I'd eaten too much Sunday dinner, but without any of the satisfaction a home-cooked meal brings.

"I've been clutchin' onto hate much like little Pat clings to his bear in the night's darkness. That can't be anymore—not for me, not for him and not for my Pat either. It's not what he'd want me to be doin' while he's off fightin'."

Daddy hugged me against his chest, strong as an ox at nearly 82. "I hope you hold on to that thought, my dear Mabel. I have something to tell you and something to ask of you. Keeping up with the demand for food with only your oldest brothers to plant, harvest and tend has been a challenge."

I knew that well. With most of our young men gone to war, local industries hurt for workers. Many of my girlfriends had taken up the hammers and work pants of their beaus and brothers. Little Pat kept me busy, but I knew I, too, might need to further support the war effort from our home front.

Daddy's explanation continued. "Hundreds of German prisoners of war will be brought to a tent camp on the old Wiley land. I'm hoping they'll allow the men to fill some of our labor gaps. While many will probably cut pulpwood, I've expressed a desire that a handful of the men be assigned to me. If possible, I'd like some with an interest in farming."

My mind reeled, struggling to process Daddy's news.

Germans, in Aiken County? Germans, on our land? The enemy ... walking, free as you please, near my son, while his father fights for his life in one half of this awful war and his uncles stare down gun barrels into the evil eyes of the very Germans Daddy wants to welcome with open arms? After all they've taken—are taking—from our family, how could Daddy consider this?

Daddy was talkin' again, this time with his hand cupping my cheek. "Mamie will need to cook breakfasts and lunches for the men. She can't take on such a task alone. I'm asking you to help her with the extra cooking and cleaning."

Thoughts fought to be spoken. Most of the words stuck in my throat like my initial failed attempt at grits. I choked out, "Surely William and George want no part of this."

I watched my brothers walk side by side in the field before us. My oldest brother gestured across the fields as he spoke. They laughed, and George steadied himself on our brother's arm before ambling farther along the rows. William always walked slower to accommodate the war injury that nearly took George's left leg.

"We talked at length last night. They have pain in their memories of Germany, but they also have good thoughts. They understand what it's like to be in a country of enemies and want to do what we can to give these men a positive experience in the United States."

My thoughts whirled, reminding me of how quickly Mamie could whisk a batter, start a roux and boil potatoes—at the same time. I fixated on another reason against Daddy's horrible plan. If nothing else got through to him, this should.

"You know they're not feedin' Nicholas good food. They're probably starvin' him. Or worse!" The tears took over, and I left Daddy with one parting jab. "You helpin' these men shames my brother's sacrifice."

I'm not proud of my response or how I stormed away to sulk the rest of that evening. The thought of Germans struttin' about our lands as though they had any right to be there turned my stomach like the hog's head cheese my Daddy loved so much. The only thing that could be worse was if they were Japanese. My hatred bubbled to the top of my heart and sizzled away the rest of the night—a searing worse than the indigestion I endured durin' my pregnancy.

Daddy's proposal offered an opportunity to do my part for the war effort and improve my cookin' for the day Pat returned. However, the thought that stuck in the front of my mind was how much the task would test my newfound desire to put away anger and hate, to forgive ... to love.

Love our enemy?

Impossible.

I tossed myself into a restless sleep and dreamed about my Pat, as I did most nights. That dream was different, though.

Pat wandered along the shores of the Pacific Ocean, a small metal bowl in his hands. He was skinnier than a beanpole and terribly haggard. He stopped ev'ry few yards and held out his bowl toward the waves.

"Won't you give me a few bites to eat? I'm hungry, so very hungry."

I woke on a pillow drenched in my sorrow. I didn't know a person could cry in their sleep.

Later, I learned that dream wasn't far from my Pat's reality. During battles, they often went without food for days on end. On Guadalcanal they received two tablespoons of rice, twice a day. The amount was bad enough. Far worse were the maggots filling the rice. The thought gives me the shivers and inspires the extra pats of butter I add to my rice now.

The mornin' after that awful dream, I hugged Daddy and said, "I'm sorry for the horrible words I spoke last night. Nicholas is much kinder and less selfish than me. He would be ashamed of me, not you. Mamie and I will make the best meals we can for those men. They are just men, after all ... far from their homes and sweethearts. Like my Pat; like my brothers."

Daddy smiled and kissed my forehead. He whispered, "Yes, child. Yes, they are."

§

Before I could reconsider my newborn charitable feelings, six Germans were assigned to work on our farm.

Their first breakfast, I carried in grits to ladle into their bowls. Most of them had the blondest hair I'd ever seen. All of them were skinnier than you'd think men of war should be. I got most of the way round the table when one of them looked up at me with eyes as blue as my Pat's.

"Danke," he said cheerfully. The smile that greeted me was kinder than I'd expected an enemy's to be.

I burst into tears and ran out of the dining room, slingin' grits along the way.

Daddy found me, hand clutchin' the pot, head on the arm slung across my raised knees and the spoon drippin' Mamie's perfectly creamy grits on the ground by my shoe. He didn't say anything, just sat right down and draped his arm across my shakin' shoulders.

When I finally stopped blubberin', I raised my puffy, tear-streaked face and attempted an explanation. "I didn't think they'd look kind."

He grinned and winked, kissed my forehead and helped me stand. "Now that we've all met, perhaps lunch will be less of a surprise."

Peter, the one whose "thank you" sent me runnin', continued to smile and thank me at every meal, though I never heard him say it—or anything else—in German again. Thank goodness he spoke English. I believe he thought his language upset me. I didn't tell him his eyes were the issue.

He was the quickest with a laugh or a joke, and watchin' him gave me hope I didn't realize I needed.

I mentioned before, I had no romantic notion of war. Daddy's frank words solidified my fear that the actions required of a man at war damaged him, deep down.

Despite my best efforts to shoo the worry from my mind as soon as it scuttled in, I wondered if the Pat who came back to me would be the Pat who'd marched proudly away. Knowin' my oldest brother still struggled showed me that a return to life as before might not be possible.

Seein' Peter smile and joke made me hope Pat could return whole after all.

§

Not all the Germans were like Peter. We hadn't even learned all their names when one of the prisoners in the camp was murdered. That incident taught us that there were Germans and then there were Hitler's Germans.

One of our workers feared he could be next, it seemed, and took his life. Some of the prisoners in Aiken were transferred to another camp for those who'd shown loyalty to Hitler's ideals. Another of the men who had sat at our dinner table was in that group.

Daddy recognized my fear as he and my brothers discussed the losses and I listened, wringing my hands. He stood and offered me his hand. We often took evening strolls through the peach orchard. Those walks are some of my fondest memories during the war's darkness.

"My sweet Mabel girl," Daddy patted my arm as we paused beneath a tree. "Don't be afraid. I won't let anything happen to you or to little Pat. Do you believe that?"

My face still remembers the smile I gave him. Though it was more genuine than I felt in the moment, that expression conveyed I knew he meant his promise. "I do, Daddy. It's just ... these events have brought the war into our home, and it raises my worries. It also makes me wonder who these men really are."

Daddy nodded and restarted our stroll. I could tell he was thinking of somethin' deep. It was the same lost-to-me look he'd get when he was surveyin' the land ahead of the spring plantin' or when he set the newspaper down in his lap to process the grim facts. Right when I decided our evening's conversation had ended, he spoke.

"Though they haven't been here long, I have had interactions with all these men. I don't claim to know their secrets or understand who they are and what they believe to be right. The events of the last few days, though, have validated my initial reactions to them. Before Günter's death and the move of the Nazis, I told the camp commander I didn't want Hans to return here. I also shared with him something I witnessed. On the second day they were in our fields, I interrupted a confrontation between those two men. They spoke in German, so I didn't understand the words. Emotions transcend languages, though. Günter feared for his life."

I put a hand to my chest as I felt a pang of sorrow for the man who had seemed younger than the others. Becomin' a mother had made me view others—even battle-hardened soldiers—in a softer light.

Daddy continued, "I don't know all the men who are still with us have been through or what they think of the war or our country or theirs. Those are things I hope to learn as I build friendships with them and we learn to communicate. What I do know is they come from a hard country. Since the War, they have lived in poverty. It seems Hitler made them promises of prosperity and of a nation worthy of pride. I also know they've been lied to by their country. They will learn those lies—like they did when they saw New York City still standing and not destroyed like the pictures they'd been shown. For the first time, they are in a country of freedom where truth can be shared. Another thing I know is I will stay near them. I will speak with them and observe them. If I have any concerns, I will not allow them in our home again. That I can promise you."

"Thank you for protectin' us, Daddy." I hopped onto my tiptoes and kissed his cheek. "And thank you for caring for these men. I pray for a man as honorable as you to watch over Nicholas."

In the deepening dark of the evening, I could only feel his responding smile. It comforted me, as his promise had.

§

The remaining men became dear friends. Little Pat amused them with his antics. They'd always stop to throw a ball his way or lift him up toward the clouds for a game of airplane. We had quite the party for his second birthday. Each of the Germans brought a gift for him—a candy or gum, somethin' small they had purchased with the canteen chits they were given each week for their work.

Pat clapped and giggled at each token. He blew out his candles, and we enjoyed every bite of the birthday cake made possible by Mamie's Great Wall of Sugar. It was the first cake I'd made on my own, and Daddy bragged about it like I'd done somethin' much more important than mix some ingredients and hover by the oven to make sure they didn't burn.

"Good food fills more than the need of hunger, my sweet Mabel girl."

His words have stuck with me all these years, and there's not a time I walk into my kitchen without calling them to mind.

As little Pat grew, he listened wide-eyed to the men talk in their thick accents about Germany. One of them, Ernst, had two children back home—one he'd never met either. Out of respect for my Pat, he taught our son to salute so he could give his father a proper American welcome home.

While his lessons were a tribute for Pat, for sure, they also signified respect for us and our country. They proved Ernst was no follower of Hitler. Similar gestures—seemingly small at a glance—held far deeper meanings ... some I didn't understand until years later.

§

When Ernst spoke of his children and his desire to return to them, I fought tears. His words always made me think of my

Pat and how I hoped he was bein' cared for wherever he was. Letters remained few and far between. I knew Pat was in the midst of many of the big battles the newspapers' headlines shouted about.

And so, I prayed.

I had written him of the Germans' arrival. It wasn't until our son's birthday letter, though, that Pat shared his thoughts on the matter.

Dearest Mabel,

When I read about Germans working the farm, I was a touch hesitant. As your husband, I'll always worry about you and your safety, especially being so far away in a place where good is buried at sea.

I'm sorry to admit I've been existing filled with hate. Hate doesn't make for a good life, though.

A buddy of mine helped me see our current times in a different way. He reminded me that the Japanese soldiers are men, same as us. They carry the same fears and desires and loyalties as we do. I believe that applies to the Germans as well.

My friend taught me a way to live without hate, despite death and destruction. He forgave and loved our enemies even at the time of his death on Guam. All of us—no matter the side—are simply fighting for our lives and families, fighting to make it home.

The atrocities of a nation don't always reflect the daily life of its citizens. I thank God that your father is caring for the Germans, and I am thankful you and Mamie are feeding them such good food. Give the men my regards and tell your father I appreciate what he's doing.

I'm sure Pat's tall as a pony already. Tell him happy birthday. I wish I could be there. Let him know his Pop loves him and can't wait to see him.

§

Germany surrendered in May 1945, but the prisoners would stay on in Aiken County for another year. With the surrender, the attitude toward the Germans shifted in our nation. Many people thought they all needed the Nazi educated out of them— whether they were Nazis or not.

Our family held a unique position because, like many of the workers Daddy'd employed through the years, the German men had become part of our team … our family. We got permission to bring two of the men—Peter, who made me cry that first day, and Friedrich, another soldier about the same age as my Pat—to church with us each Sunday.

Daddy never shared with me everything the German men told him. He told me enough to know the four men who shared our table and worked our fields had come to face the truth of what the government they'd fought for had done.

I went to set the table for lunch one day but stopped short of enterin' the dinin' room. Daddy nodded at me as I backed away from the scene of Peter sobbing against my father's shoulders. Daddy later told me the men had been shown a video of the death camps where the Germans tortured and killed Jews and others.

Peter said he had chosen not to see what was happenin' right around him in Germany. He also said he didn't want to believe the stories Rolf, the other German to work in our fields, had told him of his time in the Soviet Union. They had been ordered to kill hundreds of Jews after forcing them to dig their own graves.

While Daddy never considered sharin' most of the stories they told him, he wanted me to know the reality of what the Germans were workin' through. As they came to accept their country lost another war, they doubtless feared what they would find when they did return. They also spoke in hushed tones about the possibility of being sent to Russia instead.

We witnessed the fears, sorrows and guilt that covered our German friends, as well as their changed hearts. After church and then lunch at our house, Peter and Friedrich talked about repentance for the roles they had played in the war and a desire for forgiveness from those they had hurt. Peter spoke often about the friends he'd had as a young boy who he shunned when he joined the Hitler Youth and then the Nazi party. He wondered how they were—if they were even still alive.

With the changin' opinion of Americans toward them, the Germans experienced hatred in action; and, as their friends, so did we.

Though most of our crops went to the government, Daddy still sold what he could to local merchants. The problem was those merchants—and long-time friends—had a change of heart when Daddy didn't agree that all Germans were evil monsters who should be shot. They stopped buyin' from us.

Their reactions didn't stop there. Daddy's old Ford truck took a knife to its tires and some alterations to its paint job. One Sunday while we were in church, someone threw a brick through the back window of our Lincoln. Daddy didn't let me read the note around it.

Before long, the whole county seemed to be against us—except, of course, the Hills and Smiths. Barbara Hill and Margaret Smith, two of my best friends, happened to fall for Peter and Friedrich.

Even war can't stop love.

Thankfully, their parents supported their choices, and our families pulled tighter than a granny knot as we became outcasts together.

I suppose our protection of and friendship with the Germans seemed crazy to our neighbors, especially when my brothers returned. Charles remained mostly untouched on the outside, but Nicholas had lost more than half his weight between the German camp and his time on the Long March. That experience at the end of the war cost him a few toes.

He returned with nightmares his wife Paula did her best to wake him from with hugs and kisses, infusing love into his darkened soul.

Though they knew about the German workers, Charles and Nicholas might not have been prepared to see them sitting at our table. Daddy had long talks with them in his study. He had more in the fields with the Germans and still others with my brothers in the mix.

As the summer thawed my brothers' hearts toward the men in our company, they began to share stories from Germany with the men who missed the good of their homeland. As sharing began, the battle-weary men exchanged the pain of their living hells on earth. Regardless of nationality, all warriors have hearts and souls that must sift through everything they saw.

By autumn, they became friends, but neighbors continued to stand against us. I saw the toll our community's actions took on my aging father. Again, I fought anger and hate—this time against folks I once considered friends. Daddy didn't visit in town like he used to—no more Thursday morning checker games or Monday mornin' chats over coffee. That suited me and little Pat just fine. We had more time at home with him, which turned out to be a bigger blessin' than we could've known.

§

While turmoil brewed in our town, war still raged in the Pacific. I wondered if it would ever end and grew short on hope of Pat returnin' in one piece. It didn't help that I hadn't had a letter in a while. From following the papers, I figured he had been on Okinawa. Those articles did nothin' to ease my worries.

And then we saw the headlines:

"HIROSHIMA WIPED OUT!"

"ATOMIC POWER UNLEASHED ON JAPAN!"

My mind couldn't comprehend the horrific meanings of those words. I learned then that there would be many things about that war—and all others—that are too terrible to accept as right.

I thought of the families of our German men and imagined if it had been their hometowns. I considered it could have happened to the U.S. instead and wept for Japan's waiting wives—women like me—who never saw the bombs approach.

Despite the horrors I knew I'd never fully process, my hope was soon renewed. The headline we'd longed for finally graced our doorstep:

"JAPANESE SURRENDER ON ALLIES' TERMS!"

A few weeks before little Pat turned three, we celebrated our nation's victory in the Pacific with my first solo peach cobbler. Food had become the one good thing I could gift to those around me, and I poured my heart into every dish I prepared.

I wanted to celebrate, but the war's end tormented my mind. Also, I hadn't heard from Pat in far too long. His silence rose inside me and ground the buttery, flaky crust to grit in my mouth.

A week after another birthday party without Pat's presence, a letter arrived.

Dearest Mabel,

I'm sure you've heard by the time you get this that Japan surrendered! I just returned from the USS Missouri where they signed the papers. Boy, was it tough not to cry!

We welcomed our men who've been held as POWs by the Japanese. Thank your father again for his kindness to the Germans. Our men received none here. Many of them were unable to walk on their own from the prison where they were held, and all of them had lost most of the weight they once carried.

If nothing else, I hope this war has taught me hospitality and mercy. I pray you and I will remember these dark days and open our door to any lost soul in need of home.

There is a downside; I'm not coming right home. We're heading onto the mainland to help with some clean up and to make sure the surrender sticks. None of us really knows what to expect there, especially where we dropped those bombs.

I don't know how to process power and death like what we've shown the world.

It feels like I've been gone a lifetime, and I'm not sure I remember what a fresh peach tastes or smells like. I sure do look forward to getting reacquainted.

Far more than peaches, though, I miss you. I've missed celebrating my boy's birthdays.

I love you both and will see you soon.

The war was over, and my Pat was alive. He made it.

I repeated those sentences as my tears nearly ruined the letter in my lap. The days slowed to a crawl as I prayed and waited for news that he was finally headin' home. He could even be home for Christmas.

Surely, he would be.

October brought pumpkin pies and cooler weather. November brought Thanksgiving. Mercy! Was I ever thankful! But the dressin' stuck in my throat, and the gravy couldn't add enough moisture to the turkey. I had no idea where, exactly, in Japan my Pat was … or how much longer we'd be apart. It's hard to enjoy food with half your heart a world away.

The first of December delivered a sorrow I don't reckon any daughter can prepare herself for. When I think of losin' my

Daddy, I give thanks that he passed in his sleep after having all his livin' sons at home again during peacetime.

Between Daddy's passin' and the shift in our community's opinion of us, the farm wasn't the same. We all knew things would be different movin' forward, but none of us wanted to take steps of change yet.

As Christmas drew nearer, I took to standin' on our wraparound porch a few times each day, lookin' up the long, winding driveway and prayin'. I decided he might just show up at the front door one day, so I figured I'd keep an eye out. We'd heard returnin' heroes couldn't always get a phone call through once they made it to California, and he would certainly beat the mail.

Little Pat sensed my excitement, and it brought him comfort in those days after sayin' goodbye to my daddy. My son couldn't understand the world around us—headlines and prisoners and war and surrender and death. At the end of the day, he was a three-year-old who'd never met his father and had just lost his grandpappy.

I told him his Pop could be home most any day. He practiced his salute and, every night after his prayers, he'd kiss me goodnight and whisper, "Maybe tomorrow, Mama."

Tomorrow finally came.

§

A few days before Christmas, Mamie and I began baking in earnest. I'd kept faith that my Pat would be home to celebrate with us, so we were scoopin' deeper into our hidden stores. That mornin', I was preparing the dough for a peach cobbler and had a fine dustin' of flour on my hands and cheeks.

Little Pat came runnin' into the kitchen. "Mama! Mama! A car's comin'!"

I raced to the front porch, rolling pin in hand. When the passenger door opened and my Pat emerged, I sent that pin to flyin' and ran like I hadn't since I was a girl. He barely had time to drop his bag before I leapt into his arms. He twirled me around like he had all those years before when he told me he was a Marine Raider and I told him he was a father.

"I kept my promise, Mabel."

"I kept mine too," I whispered. "You'll have fresh-made peach cobbler tonight. Mamie says I'm a better baker and cook than she is. I'm sure she's just bein' sweet, but I have gotten pretty good at it. And, from the look and feel of you, you're in need of some fattenin' up."

I felt his arms and shook my head. "Skin and bones, you are!"

His laugh reminded me that he was my home, my comfort, my love—and he had returned. I felt a tuggin' on my pant leg. We looked down into the wide, solemn eyes of our son.

"Is this my daddy?"

"Yes, indeed! Your handsome daddy's come home to us."

Little Pat took an intentional step back. His tiny arm shot his hand up in a perfect salute—his best yet.

I don't reckon any of the workers or family circlin' us had a dry eye as father saluted back and then scooped up the son he'd waited more than three years to hold.

We feasted that night. I couldn't stop smilin' and wouldn't take my eyes off my conquerin' hero. Pat presented me with wooden cherry blossom flowers he'd whittled. He made wooden cars that became our son's favorite toys. Little Pat wouldn't go anywhere—including bed—without at least one tucked under his arm.

My Pat's new talent amazed me. When I asked him about the whittlin', he said, "I wanted somethin' to do with my hands. A few of the other Marines taught me."

I examined my husband through our first few weeks together and made some observations.

You can tell a man who's seen war. Living without promise of the next second hardens yet somehow also softens his face.

The atrocities he's witnessed—the ones he'll never describe in his wakin' hours, though his nightly screams paint a vivid enough picture—haunt his eyes.

His smile would never be the same. Sometimes that saddened me, but other moments showed me he was okay, despite everything. Pat's grin broadened when he'd lose himself in little Pat's antics. His smile spread true, and his laugh rolled—more like the ocean on a calm day than when a storm's rollin' in. In those moments, he focused on his son's joy and on the beauty of peace—all things I'd never know him to take for granted.

At a special Marine reunion years later, I learned more of what Pat had done in the war. His hand was sore from all the shakin', and my eyes were moist with the parade of kind words.

"Because of you, I came home and became a doctor."

"My Ginger and me had us six young'uns. None of 'em would be here if you hadn't stuck by me on that night of hell."

"Your courage has stuck with me all these years."

Any bitterness I carried over him missin' our son's first years vanished when I met all those who wouldn't've been without him up on that Ridge or on the other islands they watered with their blood and sweat.

Pat returned from Japan with his love for all fellow men intact. He became friends with the German workers more quickly than my brothers had. Mamie and I continued to cook for our friends until they went home the following July.

What surprised me were the tears in my eyes as we said goodbye to the men I once saw only as enemies.

Ernst was eager to return to his wife and children. Little Pat saluted him as the man had taught him. I noticed the tears as he saluted back and wondered how his own boy would greet him.

Ghosts of all he'd seen and done still haunted Rolf's eyes. We would never hear from him again, and I often wonder what he returned home to and if he ever found peace. I comfort myself with reminders of his occasional smile—never as full as Peter's, but lifted nonetheless.

My brothers eagerly signed as sponsors for Peter and Friedrich. They obtained visas and returned to marry Barbara and Margaret in a double wedding Mamie and I happily baked and cooked for. The men bought land from us to build homes for themselves and their families. Over the years, neighbors would come to loosen their hate and accept the men as part of our community.

With the closin' of the POW camp and the sale of land to our friends, my brothers and I sat down to discuss the future of our farm. They were ready to reduce their farmin' burden.

The night before, Pat and I had made our own decision.

"Would you want to continue workin' the farm here?"

Pat was quiet for a while as we lay together. He stroked my hair as I counted his heartbeats.

"Remember when I told you sweat and a sore back's the mark of a good day of work?"

"I do."

"Well, I don't reckon that's the only mark of a good day of work. I took up whittlin' to work with my hands."

"Would you want to just have our own piece of land?"

"How would you feel if we didn't?"

I could tell Pat knew exactly what he wanted to do but worried it wouldn't line up with my wishes.

"Lands' sakes, Pat! If you want to move on back to Columbia and take over your family's hardware store, I'm fine with that. Long as we're together and you don't go off to fight another war, I'd be happy in a cardboard box under a train bridge. 'Cept I'm not sure how I'd cook your biscuits and gravy in a place like that."

"I'll make sure you get a real nice kitchen."

"Then I'll make sure you have three full meals a day and a fresh dessert ev'ry night. Thanks to Mamie, we've got plenty of sugar stored to last us 'til they finally stop rationin'."

"That sounds mighty nice."

§

Pat and me left my Daddy's land a few months later to start our new life with little Pat and another child on the way.

As we drove to Columbia in Daddy's old Lincoln Continental with a few bags of Mamie's war sugar in the trunk, we talked about the people we'd met on account of the war.

Pat had found unexpected kindness on Japan, and we gained lifelong friends in the German POWs. In all cases, one side believed they knew things about the other … things that sometimes proved false—like the Japanese children believin' that to become a United States Marine, a man had to kill one of his parents.

We didn't know the full truth about our country either. American leaders made unthinkable choices with lasting consequences.

Pat and me agreed the greatest lesson of all had been to choose love over hate and to not allow the war to destroy our souls.

"If I hadn't listened to Daddy and opened my heart and mind to people who'd been our enemies, I reckon I'd be as sour as an old persimmon."

My Pat chuckled at me and said, "I sure am glad you're just like I left you, sweet as a peach, fresh off the tree."

Love & Cummerbunds

Cummerbund is a funny word.

My dad buckles mine for me. He's already got his on and looks so handsome. I wish Mom could see him.

He says the same two things to me: "You look handsome, Son. I wish your mom could see you today. She'd be so proud of you and Daisy."

I miss my mom. The tears creep out again. Dad says tears aren't a bad thing. Sometimes they come at the worst times, though—like when you're about to stand at the front of your church while your true love walks down the aisle.

Daisy is my true love. We have been best of friends since school, but I never thought she would date me ... definitely never thought she'd marry me.

When I was little, I thought about getting married—like all kids do. It was a big dream for me. As I got older, though, I figured marriage wasn't for someone like me.

Some of the kids at my school made sure I knew I wasn't like them. They used mean words when they saw me. All I wanted was to be their friend, but they decided I was too different. Some people let me be their friend, though.

Like Jack. He's one of my best friends. We worked together on the Tucker homes. Those are houses for families who don't have homes. Jack's one of my groomsmen. He came all the way from Camp Lejeune for our wedding. He's a Marine.

I'm proud of him. I remember I didn't act proud when he told me he wanted to join the Marines. That wasn't being a great friend.

"Jack! I'm proud of you being a Marine. I'm sorry I wasn't when you first told me you wanted to be one. I was worried. But, I should have been a great friend and told you then I was proud. So, I'm proud of you!"

He smiles at me. He's got a nice smile; I should tell him that, too.

"And, you've got a great smile! You're gonna make our pictures look way better with that smile."

Jack play-punches my shoulder and then hugs me.

"Ducky, you have always been a great friend. I'm happy for you and Daisy, and I'm proud to be standing up there with you today while you say your *I do*s. This is a pretty huge day. You ready?"

"I was born ready for this day, Jack!"

We all laugh. Those tears try to sneak out again, though.

I blow my nose one more time. Hands washed extra well— I sing the birthday song twice. Dad and Jack hold my tux jacket while I slide my arms in. Dad buttons it just right.

We hear a knock at the door, and Pop answers it. Mawmaw Mabel is there with flowers for our buttonholes lined up in a cardboard box lid.

She doesn't stop her tears.

"Oh, my sweet Ducky! My little lamb, all grown up. You're the handsomest groom I've ever seen ... except for maybe your daddy. You made such a good-looking model in your suit that day." She pats my dad's arm and hands Jack the box.

"Jack, don't you look a picture?" She gives him one of her famous hugs.

Hugs from Mawmaw Mabel are like being snuggled by a cloud made of her famous dumplin's. She always smells like biscuits and cobbler ... with a dash of baby powder. I've always liked that smell.

I bet she's made all my favorite foods for our honeymoon to the mountains.

"Did you remember Daisy's favorite cookies, Mawmaw?"

"Of course, Ducky dear! I couldn't forget those. I made you a fresh batch of biscuits this morning, too. And Aunt E. sent along a whole basket full of jams and jellies and preserves. I don't know where she thinks y'all are goin' or how long you'll be there, but she doesn't want you to be without your favorites, you know. Y'all just bring on back whatever you don't eat. It'll all keep in your new pantry, of course. Now, you stand still while I pin this flower on you. Yessir, just like that. This baby's breath is simply lovely behind the rosebud, don't you think? Daisy did such a good job pickin' the flowers and everything. Her dress ... breathtaking! Course, you won't have seen that yet. You will soon. Now, don't you cry a river, y'hear?"

She pulls a tissue from some hidden pocket and dabs her cheeks.

"A few tears are okay, though." She finishes with a wink and a kiss on my cheek. Then she shuffles out the door, talking all the way.

"Mary Anne would've been so proud. Oh, my Ducky ... sweet lamb ..."

Pop closes the door and chuckles. Sometimes he does that when Mawmaw walks off still talking. I think that's his way of showing how much he loves her.

They got married right before Pop went off to war, and Dad was born before Pop came home. I'm named for them. Patrick Miller—First, Second and Third. I think it's special to share a name, but each have our own, too. Everyone calls me Ducky. I love ducks.

Daisy loves ducks, too. When I asked her on a date, she said yes! So, I took her to one of my favorite places—the duck lake. We fed the ducks and talked and laughed. The ducks didn't look at us funny.

When we take dates at other places, like restaurants and movies, we get funny looks. I can tell they all know Daisy is way too good for a guy like me.

One night after a movie, we passed a group of guys about our age. One of them whistled at Daisy and another yelled, "What're you doin' with that freak, baby? When you get done freak-sitting, call me!"

I've been called that before ... and other things. I don't listen anymore ... not much, anyway. Daisy was mad, though. She wanted to tell them what she thought of them, but I asked her not to.

She listened to me and gave me a big hug. She whispered, "I'm so sorry they said those awful things, Ducky."

"What are you doing with me, Daisy? You could date any guy you want. Why me?"

She put her hand on my cheek. It was soft and warm and made me think of kittens.

"You are one of the kindest guys I've ever known. You make me happy, and you care for me. You notice when I'm sad and always cheer me up. And, I know you would never, ever hurt me. Plus, I love you, Ducky."

My heart skipped; I couldn't believe it—Daisy loved me! I told her I loved her and then … well, I gave her our first kiss. Her lips were as soft and kind as the words she said.

That day, I decided to focus on love, not hate. Names don't last. Glares and stares don't last. Love lasts.

My love for Daisy will last forever, and that's why we're all here today at Sovereign Grace Presbyterian Church. We're focusing on love.

"You ready to get hitched?" Dad laughs at his joke, but I see him fighting tears, too.

I hug him and blink a few times. "With you as my best man—you know it!"

§

My son looks dashing in his tux. I watch him talk and laugh with his friends on our way to the sanctuary for his wedding. Mary Anne would be proud for our boy today. She insisted we never treat Ducky different or less capable because he happened to have Down syndrome.

We decided to encourage his dreams. We surrounded him with love and a community of angels who looked out for him, while helping him learn to be the very best person he could be—full of love and kindness. He could pursue whatever passions he had and be whoever God planned him to be. No limits.

Though we agreed on how to raise Ducky, I was the doubter. I worried about how to parent a child with different abilities. I fretted over how people would treat him. And, I couldn't quite picture this day—my grown son in a tuxedo, walking to the front of the church to say "I do" to a kind and loving young woman.

I grin as I think of my soon-to-be daughter-in-law. Daisy's always been a friend to Ducky. None of us knew the hell she grew up in, but we all knew the kindness in her heart. When Ducky brought her home after their first date, I could see she cared deeply for him. I wasn't sure this day was in their future, but I began to hope. I knew it'd been a lifelong dream of Ducky's. He was only nine when he started praying for his "one-day wife."

"Do you have a girlfriend at school, Ducky?" Mary Anne asked him after his bedtime prayer.

"Oh, I have several girl friends. Girls are more friendly than boys most of the time."

My wife smiled at me while Ducky crawled under his covers. "That's nice, but I meant do you have a special girlfriend? You prayed for your one-day wife."

"Oh! No. I'm too young to date yet, Mama." Ducky patted my wife's hand. "I'll meet my wife one day, but she's already somewhere now. So, I should pray for her, even though I don't know her name. God knows, so He'll take special care of her until I find her."

Junior high and high school took a toll on Ducky's heart and dreams. Losing his mama when he was only ten didn't help anything. Both of us felt broken after that.

Anyway, he stopped praying out loud for his "one-day wife." I asked him about it, and he got still and quiet. I knew he'd had an especially rough time that semester with some of the kids in his classes.

Ducky finally answered. "Girls don't marry monsters, freaks, retards or dummies. I'm all those things."

I thought my heart was gonna rip clear down the middle. Knowing people were out there calling my son those names nearly made me lose my religion. All my son ever wanted was to be a friend to every person he met.

"Patrick Miller, you look at your old man. You are none of those things, y'hear me? You are a kind and generous friend, a good student and the best son I could have ever hoped for. Remember what your mama always said about you?"

I watched the tears roll down his cheeks as he slowly nodded.

"She said you were the best thing that ever happened to us and that God made you so special. He put you together in her just right, full of so much extra love and goodness. She couldn't believe God chose her to mama such a sweet boy, and I feel the same way. I love you, Son. Don't let those words push your head down. Hold it high and remember all the people who love you and who would never, ever think of you as any of those untrue things you heard. Okay?"

He nodded, and his smile soothed my fiery heart. I hugged him extra tight and prayed most of the night, while I cried like I hadn't since saying goodbye to my Mary Anne.

Now, we climb the stairs at the front of the church, and I swipe my eyes. I've never seen a bigger smile on Ducky's glowing face as he looks out at the sanctuary full of guests. I thank God for granting a young boy's prayers for his "one-day wife" as well as the prayers of two parents who only ever wanted openness and love for our son.

§

The church is packed! So many people came. Daisy told me they would come. She is usually right.

Mama always told me I had a giant circle of friends and family—people who love me. I didn't always believe her either.

Now I believe them both.

Standing in front of all these people is making me hot. I don't want to sweat. I don't want to cry either. I'm not sure which would be worse.

I look at my best man. My dad has always been who I want to be like because he is the best man I know. When I was real little, he took me with him to work and to get my favorite pancakes. Every night after Mama died, he held me while I cried myself to sleep.

He smiles at me now and hands me a handkerchief. My best man—always looking out for me!

I dab beneath my nose. The worst part of tears is they make other things leak, too. *That* would be the worst.

§

The wooden-framed mirror that holds my reflection has long been on my wish list. Ducky gifted it to me—his wedding present. In the card he tucked in the hinge, he wrote: *Thank you for seeing me. Now you can see the beauty I get to look at every day for the rest of our lives.*

I will away the tears as I examine my image. My wedding dress is straight from my dreams. Tulip sleeves over a fitted mermaid cut—the perfect ratio of satin to lace. I touch the pearls around my neck—an heirloom passed down through the women in his family ... now, my family.

The door opens, and I hear the pipe organ. Family members will be finding their seats. My bridesmaids will be making their graceful walks down the aisle. My turn will be next.

Mawmaw Mabel shuffles through the doorway. She gives me an emotion-filled hug and kiss. She cups my cheek as we swap smiles. A final squeeze of my hand and then she leaves.

I've never heard her say nothing before.

Once more, I examine my reflection. Peace, contentment, joy—three characteristics I used to never see in the mirror. Ducky exemplifies them. He is why I live in hope, not fear, and why I wake up excited every day to discover what adventures await.

People think I'm crazy. They think I'm weird or that something is wrong with me or—worse—that I'm taking advantage of Ducky.

I might be weird and have something wrong with me, but the love that Ducky and I share is as real as anything. He is my everything and makes me happy. I hope I make him happy, too; he deserves nothing less.

People don't understand us. I get that and, honestly, I don't waste time dwelling on their issues. What I don't get are the threatening letters that began arriving at the newspaper where I work once we ran our wedding announcement.

Writing has always been my passion. It helped me survive my childhood of abuse. My journals gave me both an outlet and a proof for the hell I lived through. They're what helped me understand that what my "uncles" did to me and how they told me it was our secret wasn't right or normal.

When I write now, I do it to share truth and impact positive changes. I write uplifting stories or shine light on things that shouldn't exist and need to be stopped.

The people who wrote those hateful letters ... well, I'm not sure why they felt they had to write them. They're certainly not seeking truth or goodness. My editors told me I should seek legal action against some of them. I could, I suppose. What they wrote was horrible and foul. Pressing charges on them would only drag me through more of their filth, and I had enough of that for a lifetime when I testified to put away the men who hurt me.

All my life, I've been viewed, especially by men, for what I can do and be for them. Ducky doesn't look at me that way. He sees me—the me who likes to be silly and goofy, who loves cheesy movies and music, who enjoys the little things in life. Most of all, Ducky genuinely loves me.

Love is precious. It's not something to overlook or take for granted.

I've been a reporter for four years. Through that time, I've seen much that doesn't make sense. I've seen evil, and I've seen hate. Some of the things I've seen have made me wonder how love can exist in such an awful world.

However, I've also discovered a brighter truth. Genuinely kind people are the quiet ones, the ones you have to seek out, the ones you may not notice at first. They're also the ones you won't let go of once you've found them.

Ducky is one of those people, and I have no intention of letting go of him or of taking him and his love for granted. I love his smile and the way he always looks for the good. Even when people call him names or give him ugly looks, he chooses, in those moments, to focus on something positive. He'll point out cat-shaped clouds I missed or remind me of our homeroom teacher who shared kind thoughts about every student.

Every morning, Ducky wakes up in a world full of evil and hate and chooses to see the good. More than that, he chooses to *be* the good.

He buys a new ice cream cone for the child who dropped hers in a mud puddle. He encourages the basketball player who's having an off day and missed a shot he usually makes. He notices when someone is eating her lunch alone and asks if he can join her.

Ducky is who I wish to imitate.

Above all these things, Ducky is the man I love with my whole being. He is the one I want to spend every day of my life with and the one I want to cheer up on his bad days. He's the one I can't wait to tell about my day or cook supper with. He's the one I love to take walks with and try new restaurants with.

And yes, Ducky is the most handsome man I know, in part because the light of God and His goodness radiates from him in such a way that, sometimes, I swear his face glows.

As I look once more in the oval mirror, I see a hint of that same glow and smile. Because I've seen the worst of this world, I choose to be part of its best. I'm ready to walk down the aisle and pledge myself to a lifetime of being the good with the best man I know.

§

Quiet can be awfully loud.

The giant organ stops playing, and I can feel the silence throb inside my ears. When our organist starts again, I hear the song I've been waiting for.

A sharp pain stabs somewhere between my stomach and my heart.

What if Daisy doesn't come? What if all those people who said she shouldn't be with a freak like me are right? What if she finally sees me like they do?

I feel the heat again. My heart beats like the big drums in parades when they march right next to you. It kind of hurts, and I get a little scared. I look to my best man.

Dad's smiling at me. He nods toward the back of the church, so I look that way. The doors open, and I see her.

Daisy's more beautiful than ever. That's saying something—she is always beautiful.

The sun must be behind her because she's shining. Or, maybe she's the sun. Either way, she floats toward me, like she's standing on a cloud.

That ache is gone. The heat is gone. I feel only love, joy and wonder.

Daisy reaches me, and I take her hand in mine. I lean toward her and whisper, "You look more beautiful than ever, my love."

She smiles and catches my tear on her thumb. We turn to Rev. Steele.

"Love suffers long and is kind; love does not envy; love does not parade itself, is not puffed up; does not behave rudely, does not seek its own, is not provoked, thinks no evil; does not rejoice in iniquity, but rejoices in the truth; bears all things, believes all things, hopes all things, endures all things. Love never fails."

My bride still glows.

Our love will never fail because we're loved by God. We love Him, too. The people filling this church today see and feel that love, too. It's why they're here.

Rev. Steele asks me if I do. I smile at Daisy again.

"I do!"

So does she!

We gathered here because Daisy and me, my dad and mom, Pop and Mawmaw Mabel, Jack and all the people behind us picked the best choice of all—love.

I look at Daisy. For the rest of my life, I decide to make two choices every day. I choose Daisy, and I choose love.

Rev. Steele declares, "I now pronounce you husband and wife."

Then he tells me I can kiss my bride—in church!

So, I do.

Everybody claps. Daisy laughs. We turn to all our guests, and I hold Daisy's hand.

Daisy Miller is my wife.

I'm hot again, but it's the heat that comes from being happy and excited. My heart feels so full, I wonder if it might pop. Something in there bubbles up my throat, and I can't hold it back.

I pump my other fist in the air as we walk down the aisle and yell out my favorite verse.

"Love never fails!"

Legacy of Heroism

"Blessed is the man who endures temptation;
for when he has been approved, he will
receive the crown of life which the Lord has
promised to those who love Him. ... So then,
my beloved brethren, let every man be swift
to hear, slow to speak, slow to wrath ...."
James 1:12, 19

Life Lessons in Courage & Woodworking

Early 2020: 5 years old, preschool

"Why is there war?"

I finish the whisker work on the cat I'm carving and set my tools on the workbench. Tray watches me, confident his dad's got the answer. I wonder if a day will come when I don't feel thoroughly unqualified for this mission of fatherhood.

My son returns my smile as I motion him over. He climbs beside me on the bench and adjusts the pint-size tool belt we bought him for his fifth birthday. I told Rachael it was time he had his own tools, and she agreed.

This woodshop began as mine, but it's become ours. I gaze at the spot by the glass door where Tray's bouncer used to sit. When I worked on my louder saws or taught classes, he stayed inside the shop with my mom. The rest of the time, though, he and I hung out here.

His first steps happened between the table saw and my scrap wood bin, and his first words—despite what Rachael says—were definitely *miter saw.*

It feels like an eternity since he spoke, but an eternity's not half long enough to unearth an answer for a question like his. Tray pulls on the tape measure clipped to his belt, and I know I've pushed the boundaries of time for my answer.

"I'll be honest, buddy, you asked a tough question; and I'm not sure I've got the answer for you. War's been part of life since soon after Adam and Eve ate the fruit and got kicked out of the garden."

Tray furrows his brows and rests a fist on his hip—a mannerism Rachael has pointed out he copies from me. He shakes his head and says, "Sure wish they hadn't done that."

I suppress a chuckle and nod my agreement. "I hear you! Back to your question—every war or mission that's ever been has had different causes—reasons for happening. Usually, the root is one group wants something someone else has or one group wants to stop another group from hurting people who can't defend themselves."

"Are we always the good guys?"

Another tough question.

"Well, buddy, I sure hope so. In the wars I know the most about, I believe we were on the right side or had good intentions. That doesn't mean all Americans have always done everything good and right. We're not perfect—far from it, as you'll learn in history classes. We have much in our past I wish had happened differently. I may not be able to change what happened before me, but I can work to do right today."

"Did you always do the right thing in your war?"

I run my good hand up and down the arm that will never again lift a weapon ... or much else. Memories rise but don't send me into a spiral like they would have a few years ago. I still feel the pangs of guilt and see every choice, every action, every squeeze of the trigger ... and every face lost on both sides.

Those reminders don't seem to be going anywhere, so I consider the lessons I have finally learned and which pieces of them I can share with my young son.

"I always wanted to do right, but I messed up more than my share. Everyone does."

"Will you tell me your war stories?"

I tousle my son's hair and answer this question more quickly. "I'll tell you the stories I think you're old enough to hear when we work in the shop, but I won't just tell you my stories. I know a bunch of braver warriors than me whose stories you should know. What do you think about that?"

Tray's eyes light up. He hops down and salutes. "Outstanding, sir!"

"At ease, Private Calhoun!" I salute back before leading him toward the house where Rachael calls us for dinner. "I have it on good authority that mama made us pork chops with spiced apples."

Tray races out of the shop and calls, "Come on, Scout Two!"

I chuckle at the gangly, goofy Irish wolfhound who's eerily like his father. He lopes after my son, and boy and dog run full-speed-ahead at my wife. I scoop up the little girl toddler-sprinting toward me, red curls bouncing and giggles echoing in the courtyard. Almost three and full of as much sass and sweetness as her mama and the two grandmothers she's named for, Carolina Rebekah fills our days with sunshine and warmth.

As I do daily, I thank God for this good thing—life with the family He's gifted me. I give thanks, too, for every good gift of the memories and conversations we share. I kiss Carolina's downy curls and ask God for wisdom to guide my words and timing to share the stories in my heart with my son.

§

Early 2021: 6 years old, kindergarten

"Like this."

My hand encircles Tray's hand and hammer as we tap in the first nail of a jewelry box, Rachael's Mother's Day present. A few more guided taps and my son flies solo to complete his work. He takes the smaller nails and lines them up to attach the hinges to the lid. I show him how to hammer in the end ones and then the middle ones.

"I did it!" I note the confidence in his stance, and we high-five. "I think I can do Nana's all by myself."

As I hand him another kit, I say, "That first nail is the hardest. Let me know if you want some help."

Tray intentionally separates each piece in the kit and arranges them in the order of use. This organizational skill—like most of his better qualities—comes from his mama. I am struck by how much he has grown—inside and out—over the past year. I examine him. Gone are the pudgy little boy cheeks, replaced with chiseled features. My thoughts wander to who he'll be when he grows up and how he'll see the world around him with those deep blue eyes he also inherited from his mama.

Shimmering spring sunlight streams through the double garage doors and warms the shop's front half. On mild days like this, I leave them open. On other days, we use the regular glass door. I prefer this openness and shoot up a prayer of thanks for another pleasant day. Scout prefers it, too. I laugh at the dog sprawled out in the sunshine—lips curled in a grin, legs chasing the rabbit bounding through his dream.

Tray's got the first four nails in, and the box is almost square. When he turns to me, I see a frown of confusion. "Hey dad? Was I born when you were in Iraq?"

"No, bud. I got back from Iraq in 2005, almost nine years before you were born."

"Oh, okay." Tray turns the box around, then adds, "I'm glad you're not still in the Marines."

"Why's that?"

"Well, my friend Colton's dad is in the Army, and he's been gone a long time. Colton misses him. I'd miss you if you were gone."

"I'd miss you, too; that's for sure." I squeeze my son's shoulder. "Do you remember Uncle Ducky's grandpa, Senior?"

Tray scrunches up his eyes and nose—he calls it his rememberin' face. "Not a lot. I do remember everybody being sad when he went to heaven."

"Yeah, we were. Happy for him to go to heaven—he was nearly 100, after all—but we miss him here. Anyway, Ducky's daddy was born when Senior was fighting in World War II, and they didn't get to meet each other until Junior was three years old."

"Wow! I can't imagine not knowing you for three whole years. That would be like you just meeting Carolina. Why couldn't he visit?"

"He was far away ... across the entire United States, then across the whole Pacific Ocean, then over a passel of islands. Plus, Senior was a Marine Raider, and they had a special task— push the Japanese back to their country and recover places they had stolen from others."

"I guess that was more important than meeting his son." Tray's chin drops to his chest. "Colton said his dad's job's more important than being at his birthday."

"Did Colton's dad say that?" I ask as I slide the next set of nails nearer to my son's hammer.

"I don't think so. When he said that the other day at his party, his mom put down the cake and said, 'Now, Colton, you know that's not true!' He said he knew, but I don't think he did."

If I were still serving and got shipped overseas, I'd be the one missing birthday parties, and Rach would be the one trying to give answers. As I squat beside Tray, I think about what I know of Colton's dad. He is most likely special forces, which means he can't tell his kid where he's going or how long he'll be there. Probably can't pop a birthday card in the mail either.

"I'll be honest, bud, I don't know Colton's dad all that well, but I do know dads. Nothing's more important to us than our families. Knowing what I know about Senior, I bet he wished more than anything to be by his wife—we called her Mawmaw Mabel—when she had Junior. I do know he always loved his son—even thousands of miles away. After Senior passed away, I learned more of the heroic things he did in the war. Those actions saved other boys' dads."

"Colton's dad might be like Senior then?"

I watch the relief spread across Tray's face and think of the burden my boy has carried for his friend. My response flows from a smile as wide as I can make it. "I bet he is."

Tray taps in the final nail. "Can we pick out some girly-colored paint now, Dad?"

"You got it!"

§

Late 2021: 7 years old, first grade

"I've been wondering something, Dad. We've got a military to fight wars, right?"

I hand Tray another sheet of sandpaper and watch him carefully smooth the wood, like I taught him.

"That's a big part of what they do."

He stops sanding. "But not all?"

"Having a strong military all the time discourages others from attacking us."

While Tray continues his sanding, I cross to the belt sander. I run my good hand around a larger piece of wood destined to become a headboard. We work silently for a while. Once I turn off the sander, I crouch eye-level with the surface and check for imperfections.

Perfect.

I listen to one of my favorite sounds—the *scratch-scratch, scratch-scratch* of sanding. The noise symbolizes a removal of roughness, an addition of uniformity and a guarantee that the wood will be straight and smooth for any future purpose. The sound stops, and my son speaks.

"Why not just make a military when it looks like something bad will happen?"

"Well, bud, that's not something we can always know. The Japanese attacked our military ships docked at Pearl Harbor in Hawaii. Terrorists hijacked planes and flew into the towers in New York and into other important places on 9/11. No one could have predicted exactly what happened on those days. The thing is—because we live in a world where people are often angry and looking for a fight—war or an attack can happen any moment."

I imagine the wheels in Tray's head spinning and sticking on fear over a looming attack. The next image is Rachael's disapproval of instilling fear in our son, so I quickly continue.

"Thankfully, we live in a country with a strong military that's ready to fight at a moment's notice. They train so we don't have to be afraid. I don't know about you, but that makes me feel safe."

Tray's smile assures me that my words have the right effect … and will keep me out of the doghouse with Rach, which is good since we don't have a doghouse. Scout and, now, Scout Two have always slept with us. More likely, she'd kick me out to the shop and Scout Two would commence drooling on my pillow instead of the quilt over my shoulder.

"I feel safe because you're my dad. Bad guys would be stupid to try and get past you."

My son's words draw moisture to the corners of my eyes. Since there's a no-crying-in-a-woodshop rule, I laugh and pretend to box with Tray. A few imaginary right hooks and he's got me down for the count.

We cross the concrete floor to my mini-fridge and pull out our favorite sports drinks—red for me, blue for him. Scout laps noisily from his water bowl and raises a dripping beard to grin at us. I inspect Tray's work and point out two missed spots. They weren't easily noticed; he's improved over the past few months.

"You know, I'm proud of you. You've done a great job learning to sand. You take your time and do the work right. When you take pride in what you produce, people notice."

"Like how people come to our shop to buy your furniture because they know what a great job you do."

I tip my bottle to tap his, and we gulp. Scout plops between us and rests his giant head on my foot. A few seconds of even breathing and he's snoring away.

Tray shakes his head at our dog's laziness. He asks, "Since you didn't grow up with a dad, how'd you learn the lessons you teach me?"

"I may have not had my dad around much when I grew up, but I had other men in my life. Senior taught me to do everything I know with woodworking. When I was younger, we were always close with Mama's family. Her dad—your grandpa—stepped in when my dad left. He went to my ballgames and tossed the ball with me."

"Was that when Mama Carolina was still alive?"

I nod my head. "Yep. And after she went to heaven, too. He was always there for me, even when I was a stupid kid."

Tray's eyes widen at my admission.

"That's right, bud; I wasn't always the wise guy you see before you today."

He rolls his eyes.

I survey the shop and notice evidence of us walking through the sawdust I should probably sweep. The trail reminds me of the yellow footprints I stood on when I arrived on Parris Island for Boot Camp. I recall my earlier conversation with Tray and add another thought.

"You know, bud, always having a military is also good for the folks who join. I was a walking disaster when I enlisted. My past held a lot of pain and many mistakes. My future was a total blank; I had no idea what to do with my life. Becoming a Marine gave me a purpose—a great one. Of course, I know now that following Christ is a greater purpose than being a Marine. Joining the Marine Corps, though, showed me how to live for a reason."

"And now, your reasons are me, Mama and Carolina."

"You're right about that, buddy. You three are a gift I give thanks for every single day."

"We're your One Good Thing—something to thank God for every day, like Mama Carolina wrote in her letter to Mama?"

"You know it!"

"You and Mama are my Two Good Things."

"I love you, bud."

"I love you, Dad."

I suppose that no-crying rule could be more of a guideline.

§

Early 2022: 7 years old, first grade

"Do you have a best friend, dad?"

Tray's sweeping skills have improved. The pile of sawdust in the middle of my shop steadily grows while I stain two new rocking chairs.

"I've had a bunch of best friends." My shadow stops sweeping, surprise arching his eyebrows, so I elaborate. "Let's see. There's your mama—she's my bestest of best friends. Then there's your grandpa and your nana. I've got Uncle Ducky and his daddy. There's Mr. Jed and Rev. Randy. Even though they're not still with us, I had Senior and, of course, the man you're named for, Trayvon."

"You can have a bunch of best friends? Marcia Mae in my class laughed when I said I had lots of good friends. She said everyone in first grade should have one *best* friend. She's got one. Her name is Laura, but I don't think Marcia Mae's very nice to her."

I nod my head as I catch a spot I'd missed with the stain.

"Being a good friend is something we have to learn. We also have to learn how to tell if someone's a good friend for us. When your mama and I were in school, I had a whole class full of friends ... or so I thought. Turned out, none of them were true friends. When things got tough—when I made mistakes and had trouble being a good friend—your mama was the only one who stuck by me. She could've left me, too, but she didn't. She was my first true friend. Being there, even when I didn't deserve it, made your mama and Trayvon special friends. They never gave up on me."

I set down the stain-covered rag and wipe my hands on another. "As far as what Marcia said to you about needing one *best* friend: in my experience, you can never have too many good friends. Some are more special to us than others; and that's how we get the whole 'best friend' thing. But, I love all my friends and try to make sure they know how much they mean to me. I want to be a good friend for them, like they are to me."

Tray sweeps again—back and forth, back and forth—even though there are no more stray shavings.

"When you were in the Marines, were all those guys your best friends, too?"

"In one way or another, yes. We were like brothers. We were willing to fight together and protect each other because that's what brothers do. But, just like brothers, we all had different likes and dislikes. Trayvon and me both loved to shoot and whittle. When we weren't training or running, Trayvon and I would almost always still be together since we enjoyed the same activities. It's not that I didn't like the other guys; we just weren't as close as I was with Trayvon. When we were in Iraq, all of us looked out for one another and hung out sometimes, but it was Trayvon I looked forward to hanging out with when we returned to the States."

"Do you miss him?"

"Every day, big guy. Every single day."

"Was he a good fighter?"

"Trayvon was one of the best Marines I've ever known because he loved others more than himself. He was kind and caring and looked for ways to help. He knew when I was having a tough day and would tell a joke or sing some goofy song. No matter how hard I'd try to ignore him and stay grumpy, he always made me laugh."

"I would have liked him! I try to do that for my friends, too."

"Then you're an amazing friend—just like him!" I drape my arm around his shoulder and wink. "We named you right."

§

Late 2022: 8 years old, second grade
"Hey, Dad!"

Tray races into the shop one afternoon, snack in hand. Scout snorts himself out of a deep sleep to sit expectantly at his buddy's feet. He always perks up at the chance of a chip falling his way.

"Hey, bud! I see Nana's fixed you up with something tasty. How was school?"

"It was okay, except ... my friend Marcus is sad."

I stack up the slats I prepped and sit beside my son on the work bench.

"Well, that's not good. Why's he sad?"

"Some of the older kids got in his face and started yelling. One said, 'Your people are causin' problems in this country.' Another said, 'Call me a racist—I dare you.'"

I picture Tray's polite, funny friend. They've been best buds since kindergarten. Marcus had me rolling last week with a whole string of jokes he memorized to share with me. I shake my head at the cruelty he experienced.

"Those boys had no business saying such hateful things to Marcus."

"I got mad when I saw them in his face, so I told them to leave my friend alone. They called me a name I didn't understand, but I know it was a bad thing to say. That happens sometimes with the older kids; they'll say words I don't know. Like ... what's a racist?"

"Well, buddy, a racist thinks they're better than another person and is hateful to them because their skin's a different color."

"All those words and that yelling were because Marcus' skin is darker than ours?"

"I'm afraid so."

"But, Dad, that's stupid. We're alike in every other way. We love to trade baseball cards and talk about the Braves. We play ball together; our favorite lunch day is even the same—cheeseburger Wednesday."

"I agree with you, buddy. You know, me and Trayvon were like you two, and that didn't keep us from being best friends. Unfortunately, many folks only see a person's skin or something else on the outside. I think a big part of the problem is people don't want to get to know others."

My son nibbles his chips and shares a couple pieces with Scout. I recognize in him my preference for silence over conversation while thinking something through and allow him a moment longer before I speak.

"I'm proud of you for standing up for your friend. Too many people aren't interested in being friends, and some don't stop with mean words. They use their fists to show their hate."

As Tray ponders my words, I return to the slats I stacked earlier. "Wanna help me put this bench together?"

"Let's do it!" He runs after me while Scout takes ownership of the empty chip bag.

"You can be my other arm. Can you hold these legs up like this while I shoot in some nails?"

"Aye, Aye, Sir!"

Scout's snores resume. He must have thoroughly licked inside the chip bag. As we work, I think about all Trayvon taught me beyond friendship and decide what more to share with my son.

"Trayvon told me that being a friend is great, but he helped me understand the mean things he experienced and fears he had were things I had never faced. He taught me that, some places we went, he wouldn't be treated the same as I would—all because of the color of his skin. Understanding that, I was able to empathize with him." Tray frowns when I drop the bigger word. "Do you know what that means?"

The shake of his head confirms my suspicion. "To empathize with someone is to understand you can't know exactly what they're going through because you're not them, but you will listen and do your best to imagine what they're feeling like so you can be a better friend every day. Trayvon helped me learn how to do that."

My son releases the leg we finished and steps back, as if considering the new word from all angles. "I want to emp-tha-tize for Marcus. He deserves a friend like you were."

"I'm proud of you for wanting to be that for Marcus. You know, he reminds me of my friend. Trayvon never let other people's mean actions stop the good he did. I've told you before how kind he was. He always looked for the best in others and for ways to be helpful." I remember the pictures of Trayvon with his grandfather in Grandma Ethel's house. "I think he learned that from his grandpa. Did I ever tell you about him?"

While Tray shakes his head, I demonstrate how I need him to hold the next leg.

"No? Well, I'll have to fix that! His name was Edwin Henry, and he was a Marine, too."

"Really?"

"Yep! He was one of the first black Marines. During World War II, President Franklin Roosevelt signed something called an Executive Order that said African Americans could join all branches of the service, including the Marine Corps. The downside was they continued to segregate—which means separate—blacks from whites. So, that's how the Montford Marines came to be."

"Why were they called the Montford Marines?"

"They had to train and live in a different place from white Marines. That place was called Montford Point."

"Did they go to the same war?"

"They did."

"Did they fight on the same side?"

"Yep."

"They couldn't live in the same buildings, though?"

"That's right."

"That's stupid."

"I agree. It didn't seem stupid to some people in our country, though."

"What did Trayvon's grandfather think about it?"

"Well, I never got to meet him, but from everything his grandson told me, Mr. Henry was excited to fight for his country as a Marine. He saw it as a chance for people to see that skin color didn't make a person any more or less brave. He lived to see his grandson graduate from Boot Camp in Parris Island, just like I did."

Tray tilts his head, much like Scout when he's curious. I listen for his question. "Why would his grandfather want to fight for a country that didn't like him?"

"That shows you how kind he was, doesn't it? Grandma Ethel talked to us about that one day during Sunday dinner. Her sweet potato pie might be the best thing I've ever put in my mouth." My stomach rumbles as I remember her melt-in-your-mouth crust and perfectly spiced filling. "Anyway, she asked him the same question. He told her, no matter our nation's past and no matter the hate and unfairness that existed, he looked forward to a different future—one where his children could be whoever God created them to be. He told her our country needed to stay free and peaceful to achieve that future, so he wanted to help with that."

"Did Grandma Ethel feel the same way?"

"I know she did later. She told us she prayed they'd tell him to go away because he was too old when he went to enlist. She said she even had a speech ready to cheer him up—how he wasn't too old for her and how she loved him anyway ... something sappy like that—with a side of sweet potato pie, fresh from the oven."

"But they didn't tell him he was too old?"

"Nope. All the guys he served with called him Pop. He was like a dad to some of them. He became their chaplain, too, which meant he was like a preacher. He prayed with and for them and talked with them about the Bible."

We work for a while and complete the frame for the bench. Tray is laying out the slats for me when he stops mid-motion and asks, "You said he was in World War II, right? Isn't that the same war Senior fought in?"

"That's right, bud."

"Did they know each other?"

"I don't think so, but Senior told Trayvon and me about the Montford Pointers they met on Guam. How about I pull together some of the stories Trayvon told and Senior told and see if we can't get a better idea of what Mr. Henry might have experienced?"

"Yeah!"

I shoot the final nails into the slats Tray's arranged for me. He helps me ease the bench off the table for the wood glue to dry.

"Like I told you, Mr. Henry wanted to serve his country, and he wanted to do it with the best branch. So, naturally, he chose the …"

"Marines! Hoorah!"

"Hoorah!" I laugh and picture Tray as a tiny baby in the Future Marine camo onesie Rachael bought before he was born.

We sit on stools I made for a customer. Scout rests his head in my lap. I scratch behind his ears and mentally sort through years of Marine history I've studied and stories I've heard.

"Mr. Henry was one of the first volunteers to arrive at Montford Point, so he had finished his training before the end of 1942 and was ready to fight. The problem was, he'd become an unofficial chaplain. The white officers saw the good he was doing with the men there—keeping them calm, encouraging them, helping them prepare for war and separation from their families—and kept him at Montford Point.

"Trayvon read letters his grandparents wrote back and forth during that time. His grandpa wrote about doing 'God's work.' He loved the men he met and the opportunity to encourage them, but he was 'tired of watching God's work march on out the gates without him.'"

"He was funny!"

"I think he's where Trayvon got his humor."

Scout lifts his furry head, and we laugh at his lop-sided, smushed beard and the puddle of drool on my pants leg. Tray grabs a shop towel for me to mop up the slobber. Before I get far, Scout drops his head back down on the towel. I shake my head at his renewed snoring.

"Like I said, they didn't send him to the war right away. It wasn't until they started putting together the depot and ammo companies that Mr. Henry told the officers how he was feeling. Now, I should probably tell you they'd already sent a bunch of fighting guys overseas. These new companies would move all the materials—especially the ammunition—up to the front lines where the fighters needed it. Some of them were bummed because they figured they wouldn't get to do any fighting. The crazy thing we know now, looking back, is the fighting Montford Marines ended up not seeing much action while the helper companies found themselves smack dab in the middle of the battles."

"Did Mr. Henry end up in a battle?"

"He sure did … one of the toughest ones. He convinced the officers that the men needed a chaplain even more when they landed in a war zone, so they put him in the 2nd Marine Ammunition Company. Mr. Henry traveled across the world. He landed on an island called Guadalcanal around the same time Senior would have gotten back there. The Raiders and others had fought hard to take that island about a year and a half before then. It probably felt good to Senior that they were heading back to a place we still controlled, thanks to their fighting."

"So, they could've met then?"

"It's likely they at least passed one another or even fought near each other because Mr. Henry's ammo company and another Montford ammo company joined Senior's new brigade to head to another island—Guam. They had no idea what would happen there. Of course, they knew from how hard it had been to take the other islands that it wouldn't be easy."

I think about how to best describe the process of landing on and fighting for an island. As I gaze across my shop, I see tools and materials as potential visual aids.

"Bring that big board over here for me."

Tray jumps off his stool and runs past my table saw to another workspace near my lathe. Scout pops his head up again.

"This one?"

"Yep! Thanks, bud. Let's put it up here." He sets the board on the table where we assembled the bench, and I take advantage of not being pinned beneath Scout to join Tray. "We'll pretend it's the island of Guam. What could we use as LSTs?"

"What are LSTs?"

"That stands for Landing Ships, Tanks. They're what the Marines rode toward the beaches. The ships also carried gear and supplies and even the LVTs—Landing Vehicles Tracked. From the bigger ships, they sailed each LST close to the beach, dropped a big ramp and these cool LVTs rolled out, through the water and onto land."

"They drive in the water *and* on land?" Tray's expression reveals awe when I nod. He scans the shop and spots stacked blocks ready for my whittling class next week. "How about these for the LSTs? Then, can we use these smaller blocks for the LVTs?"

I give him a thumbs-up as he points toward the scrap heap he'd swept the day before. "Outstanding! Bring over maybe four or five of the big ones and a few more of the smaller pieces. Now, what could we use for our Marines?"

Tray's eyes survey the shop again. "Wood screws?"

"Those will work. Put some on top of the LSTs and LVTs and set a few others down in the water."

"What about on the beach?"

"Definitely. Plus, put more further inland for the Japanese." We arrange our makeshift battle scene, and I continue where I left off, despite Scout's snores. "When they landed on the southern beaches, I imagine Senior clutched his rifle tight and adjusted his helmet as he prepared to fight."

Tray designates a larger screw as Senior and marches him and a line of his fellow Marines up onto our representation of Guam.

"Trayvon's grandpa told him that he prayed aloud as they neared Guam and continued praying as they landed and began the challenge of getting ashore. His grandpa told him that verse, 'Pray without stopping,' took on a whole new meaning in war. He and his fellow Montford Pointers had to lug stockpiles of ammunition from the water while the Japanese fired all around them. It was up to them to keep the other Marines from running out of ammo. If they didn't, it would be bad for them all. They had to be courageous."

As I talk, Tray acts out the scenes—Mr. Henry praying on top of one of the LVTs as it rolls out of the LST toward the beach, then a whole group of them unloading "ammo" (wood shavings). From there he moves the figures forward, a little at a time. I think back to the history I studied during my time in the Corps. Each yard on that island was hard-earned, and my son's reenactment is remarkably solid.

"They had to battle the island as well as the enemy. They had huge hills to overcome—which wasn't easy when the Japanese were on top and saw them coming. They fought through swamps. The ammo guys had to pass through all that tricky terrain, too, with their arms full of supplies, often through a rainstorm of bullets. At times, they picked up rifles and fought to keep going. They also carried the wounded to safety. Mr. Henry told Trayvon that he tried to carry double the load back that he did forward. He felt strongly about the Marine's understood rule of 'No man left behind.'"

Tray commandeers bits of used sandpaper for his Montford Marines to carry their wounded.

"Without the bravery of the Montford Marines, we might not have recaptured Guam or its important airfield that had been taken from us at the beginning of the war. The commander of the 1st Provisional Marine Brigade agreed and awarded them, and the white Marines they fought with, the

Navy Unit Commendation—a special award for any whole unit that shows extra bravery and fearlessness in their actions. Senior told Trayvon and me that there was no white or black in that battle. They were Marines, Americans—brave and victorious."

I notice there's no longer separation between the original groups of Marines Tray set up, and the Japanese have retreated to a far corner of our imaginary Guam.

Tray asks, "Did that make things better for them? Did they get to live with the other Marines then?"

"Not entirely, to answer your first question. And, not yet, for your second. Trayvon told me how someone called the police on his grandpa when he returned home from the war in his uniform because they thought he was pretending to be a Marine. Lots of folks didn't know there were black Marines. Shoot! I didn't know anything about the Montford Marines until he told me."

I picture the pride that shone from Trayvon's face and remember the passion that rang in his voice when he told me about his grandfather.

"He also talked about how his grandpa calmed tensions later on Guam where his unit stayed to support new troops—folks who hadn't fought beside them and hadn't seen their courage or how important they were to the victory. Mr. Henry spent the remainder of his time promoting peace and friendship among the troops. He effected change in some, but some people's hate runs too deep to be cut out. Back to your second question: it was a few years after the war before the Corps started to house and train all Marines together. It took even longer—and a couple more wars—to be how it is today."

"Why do people still hate others because their skin's different?"

"Buddy, I wish I knew. I think it goes back to what I said earlier: people don't want to get to know someone who looks different. They aren't willing to be like you and Marcus. You each carried a pocket full of baseball cards, and that brought you together, didn't it?"

"Yep! We each had an extra card the other didn't, so we swapped. Then we talked about the Braves. And then ... well, then we were friends."

My son shrugs as he explains the simplicity of something our world fights wars to solve.

I express a deep desire. "I wish more people would discover how much they have in common. We could do amazing things in our world if more of us came together as friends."

Tray sits quietly for a minute, pouring a pile of wood shavings from one hand to the next. "How can I help Marcus? Do you think those older guys would try to hit him?"

"Honestly, I don't know if they would, but I do know we need to do what we can to make sure that doesn't happen. Did you and Marcus tell your teacher what happened?"

"No. Marcus said he didn't want to think about it or talk about it with anybody."

"I tell you what, buddy. Today's Friday, so let me and Mama call Marcus' folks and invite them over to grill out tomorrow. Maybe we can work together to make sure those boys don't cause more trouble. Maybe we can even think of a way to help everyone in your school get to know each other deeper than what's on the outside."

"Can we have hot dogs and steak kebabs?"

Scout perks up and sticks out his tongue.

"I think we can make that happen."

Scout stretches and shakes himself.

"And banana pudding for dessert?"

I laugh at Scout's insistent bark in favor of pudding and reply, "Mama should be done teaching her last fitness class. Let's pick a couple flowers and head over to ask her."

"Good idea! I'll race you!"

§

Late 2023: 9 years old, third grade

"Curses!"

I chuckle as one of my wife's words of frustration launches from our son's mouth. I look toward the back of the shop in time to see Tray chuck the broom against the wall with all the force his left hand can muster. As he wheels around, I see a mirror of my own rage and sigh; children copy everything.

"Buddy, what's got you steamed up?"

"It's this dang hand! I can't do nothin' with it, and I can't sweep with one hand; it's just too hard." He kicks at the scattered sawdust. "And, it's stupid that I cut myself. I knew better, but I cut myself anyway. I can't sweep and I can't whittle and I can't do much of anything. This woodshop thing just ain't for me."

I sit on one of a pair of benches along the wall and pat the space beside me. Tray stomps over and plops on the end farthest from me. I let the stillness hang thick for a few moments. He is my son, after all; sometimes we need a breath or two before we're able to hear truth and wisdom.

As I wait, I imagine the memories that will be made around these benches and their matching table. Examining the details I put into the custom-built set, I recall when I thought I'd never build pieces like these again.

"Did I ever tell you how I felt when I learned I'd never use this arm all the way again?"

I watch Tray's chin lift an inch or so and notice the slight shake of his head, so I lean back against the wall and dig up more memories.

"Well, I was mad at the world. Shooting was my life, my purpose. I figured if I couldn't shoot like I'd done for years with this right arm and hand here, then I was good for less than nothin' and decided I'd just run away from everything."

Tray turns toward me. "You ran away?"

"I hate to admit it, but I did. It wasn't a wise decision, and I'm embarrassed I made it."

He lowers his head again and mumbles, "I didn't know grown-ups do things they're embarrassed about."

"Unfortunately, we do. The important next step, though, is to learn from our bad actions. If we don't, we'll keep making the same mistakes."

"What did you learn?" Tray slides closer and picks at the bandage covering his stitches.

"After a lot of running, I finally learned I couldn't let my arm's limitations keep me from doing something with my life. I thought about the thing I loved nearly as much as shooting—woodworking and building furniture. Senior taught me before I joined the Marines."

"Sometimes I forget you've only got one good arm. You make everything look easy."

I smile as he inches closer. "I'll tell you, buddy, that was not always the case. You should've seen me when I started re-learning. I was living on the mountain then."

"You lived on a mountain? Was that where Scout One found you?"

Scout Two raises his head from the floor, and I notice the sawdust coating his damp beard. He sucks in his panting tongue and tilts his head, intent on further mentions of his dad.

"It sure was. By the time that big goofball dog found me, though, I was getting less clumsy. I'd been working on my skills for a couple of years, so he missed me slicing into my leg on one of my earliest attempts."

"Ouch!"

"Yeah, it wasn't my shining moment, but thankfully I didn't cut anything vital to living."

Tray slides a few inches closer and leans forward, arms resting on the tops of his legs like I often do when I'm pondering something. Finally, he straightens. "Cutting my hand taught me that it will be a long time before I'm so good, I don't need to slow down and think through the safety rules you taught me."

He looks at me, and I nod.

"Word of wisdom? I haven't reached that point yet." I watch my point sink home before I press our impromptu life lesson further. "Did trying to sweep with your left hand teach you anything?"

Tray sits right beside me now, and I watch as he lowers his head to consider the past thirty minutes.

"I learned that maybe I shouldn't say 'I can't' before I really try."

"It took you a whole lot less time to learn that one than I did. I spent years stubbornly sticking to my can'ts."

I think back over my years of running, of refusing to shift who I was and of choosing instead to focus on what I'd lost … and what I thought I'd lost.

"Dad? Thanks for not sticking with your can'ts."

I smile and hug my son. As I recall his earlier outburst, I whisper, "One more word of wisdom, bud: don't say 'ain't' in front of your mama."

§

Early 2024: 9 years old, third grade

"Have you ever been scared?"

Tray's voice sounds small in the deafening silence that follows the whirr of my angle grinder. I wipe my forehead. It's hot for early April.

"Many times."

My brief response kickstarts what I predict will become a deeper discussion, so I lift two bottles of water from the fridge and lead my son to a couple of rockers I completed earlier in the week.

"I was scared senseless every time I asked your mama to date me; yes, there was more than once and, for some reason, she said yes every time. Even though I knew her answer, I was shaking in my boots when I asked her to be my wife. Then, there's you. You've scared the mess out of me more times than I can count."

"Me?"

"Yes, sir! When I found out I was going to be a dad, I knew I was going to mess up. Then, when you were about to be born, I got myself all worked up, thinking of all the things that could possibly go wrong. When you started to crawl, I was terrified you'd tumble down the stairs from our apartment into the shop and have one of my bookshelves fall on top of you. When you started eating solid foods, I feared you'd choke to death. When you started school, I was scared of you being out of my sight for so long every day."

"I'm not gone *every* day, Dad."

"True. Parents freak out over everything, though. It's part of being a mom or dad. And, don't even get me started on how scared your sister's made me!"

Tray shakes his head and grins. I lean the rocker forward, flip on the box fan and angle it toward us. Tongue lolling, Scout pads over and sprawls out in front of the cool air.

"When Trayvon and I headed to Iraq, we were scared to fly on the giant plane they loaded us into. It was nothing like the kinds of planes you ride in for vacation. It was crazy bumpy, and we were strapped to the sides of this giant open space with vehicles and equipment. I thought for sure I was going to barf into my helmet."

My son shoots me a lopsided grin and scrunches up his nose. "You had to barf in your helmet?"

"Well, they didn't provide barf bags, you see. We didn't have anything else except our hands, and those were holding the helmets, so ...." I lift my hand, palm up.

Tray rolls his eyes at my explanation. Scout has cooled off enough to sleep. He rolls onto his side and commences snoring.

"I think the first time I was ever truly terrified was when Trayvon and I went out on our first mission in Iraq. Our task was to keep the Iraqi people safe so they could vote. We had to constantly keep an eye out for the bad guys, especially their snipers."

"They could get shot for voting?"

"Yep, they didn't have the freedoms we take for granted here. Having elections was a big deal for them. I could tell they were scared, too."

"Did they tell you?"

I shake my head.

"We didn't speak the same language. I saw the fear in their eyes, but I also saw determination. When they looked at us Marines, I saw thankfulness. That was a gift from them to us, even though they didn't know it. Their gratitude boosted our bravery."

I see concern etched on my son's typically carefree face and know he hasn't had his real question answered yet, so I ask him one. "Is there something that scares you?"

He nods and studies the concrete floor and the twitching, snoring Scout. Finally, just ahead of a broken sob, Tray blurts, "I'm afraid of losing you and Mama."

"Oh, bud!" I slide my arm around his shoulders and pull him closer, despite the armrests of our rockers. "Your mama and I have no intention of going anywhere. What's got you worried about that?"

I see the unshed tears as he looks up to answer. "Landon, in my class, his parents both died in a car crash. Now, he's an orphan. I never thought about how that could happen."

As sobs shake his small frame, my son leans his head onto my shoulder. I press my cheek against him while Scout rests his chin on Tray's knees.

I think about how we're never promised tomorrow and ask God to soothe my son's fears and keep Rachael and me safe and well throughout our children's growing years. I ask for the great gift of watching them become the man and woman God plans them to be.

Once Tray's wails subside to sniffles, I kiss the top of his head and slide to my knee beside Scout. I look into my son's eyes and speak candidly.

"I cannot promise you that something like that won't happen. I just can't; and it would be wrong for me to. What I can promise you is that as long as I'm on this earth, I will hold you when fears come. I can also promise you that God will never, ever leave you a complete orphan. He will always be with you, just like He's with Landon right now. He's also promised to send peace and comfort when terrors fall on us, like they have on you today."

My son leans forward to rest his head on my shoulder as I pray again, this time for wisdom.

"What we can do every day is enjoy the time we spend together. What do you think about that?"

Tray faces me. A glimmer of light has returned to his expression. "That sounds like a good idea. Maybe tonight we can watch a movie and share a bowl of popcorn. Then, maybe we can snuggle?"

"Copy that! I'm certain Mama and Carolina will be on board with that plan." Scout's bark forces us to cover our ears. "So is Scout!"

§

Late 2024: 10 years old, fourth grade

"Today in school, we had to write an essay about what we want to be when we grow up."

Tray twists in another screw on the planter he's been building for Rachael's Christmas present. He's gotten much quicker and more confident with his screwdrivers over the past few weeks.

"Oh yeah? What did you write?"

"I want to be a Marine."

"Outstanding! Did you have to give reasons for wanting to be a Marine?"

"Yeah. I want to be a Marine so people will wave flags and salute when they see me because I'm a hero."

The confidence in his smile almost keeps me from setting him straight.

Almost.

"I've gotta be honest with you, bud, being a Marine isn't all flag-waving and cheering. It's mostly blood, sweat and tears. Also, heroes aren't always welcomed when they return home."

His shock at my final statement stands out, like the crooked screw sticking from the board in his hand. "They're not?"

"Not always or by everyone."

My buddy Harvey Rendall comes to mind. He volunteered with the Marines in 1968 at age eighteen. He'd been a top-notch rifleman but decided to get out after twenty years in the Corps and open a shooting range near Lejeune, where Trayvon and I spent most of our leave time. Harvey told us countless stories of Vietnam's jungles. Most of them aren't ones I'll be able to share with my son for many years. Others are ones I hope to never need to share. Harvey prepared us for the worst of war ... and after.

"The Vietnam War came at a time when lots of people didn't think we should've been over there fighting; and some felt so strongly about it, they threw their rage at our returning heroes. Marines and soldiers coming home from a horrible war were greeted with mean words, at the very least. Sometimes people even threw things at them or spit on them."

"Why would people do that? That's awful!"

"I agree, buddy." I help him remove the crooked screw and replace it with one he drives in straight and true. Once he sets up the final screw, I continue.

"The other truth about heroes is that sometimes the greatest ones don't have people who know and share their stories. Often folks join the military when they're young. If they die while serving, they may not have family—like children—at home to remember them."

"I never thought of that before. I guess I figured everyone's got a family."

Tray stores his tools and moves the planter to a drop cloth on the floor. He'd set a can of stain and rag there earlier. I watch as he stains the box like he's done it by himself a hundred times instead of a dozen. He is maturing and growing before my eyes. I consider my weekend plans and how it might be time for him to join me.

"You know, this Saturday, I'm joining some friends to pay our respects to a Marine from Savannah who died during WWII. They didn't find his body until recently. He wasn't married when he left, and his parents and siblings passed away long ago. We're going to his funeral to say goodbye and remember what he did. A grenade was thrown into the foxhole next to his in the middle of the night. He threw himself on top of it and saved the lives of the men around him."

As I speak, Tray's hand slows to a stop. He leaves the rag on the planter's side and stands to face me. "Dad, can I go with you? I'd like to know more about him."

"I think that's a great idea, and I'm glad you want to hear his story."

Tray wipes his hands on a clean rag as he verbalizes the thoughts developing in his mind.

"Everybody should have somebody to remember them. I can be a memory keeper for heroes who don't have family to share their stories."

I extend my fist for a knuckle bump with Tray because I don't trust my voice to move beyond the lump stuck in my throat.

We'll be memory keepers together.

§

Late 2025: 11 years old, fifth grade
Thwack!

Tray's jacket crumples to the ground after sliding down the wall he slings it against as he races into the shop. His cheeks flash as rosy as Rachael's when she's fired up about something, and I rub away a laugh under the pretense of smoothing my beard. I consider his current emotions might put our drill lesson on hold.

Scout Two lifts his snout and sniffs the situation. Scout Three runs from behind Tray and scampers to jump around his dad. The older dog nudges the pup away and walks gingerly to his bed beside my main worktable. Seconds later, familiar snores fill the workshop.

The youngster lopes back to Tray as my son advances to the drill where he gathers the tools of the day, anger evident with each motion. When he stands beside me, I return his stare and lean back against one of the high stools that have become popular sellers in the store.

"Before we can start our lesson, you're going to have to set that stuff down and tell me what's got your britches bristled."

I choose to ignore the unnecessary *thunk* of my drill on the table and wait for my son to wrangle his stampeding feelings.

"Why should I be nice to people who are mean to me?"

A heavy question, for sure—and one that requires an in-depth discussion. Tray's words drift with the sawdust for a few moments while his anger slowly settles. Scout Three looks from me to Tray and back.

Tray's sigh lingers as he gathers the words to express context for his emotional state.

"Most of the kids in my class are okay. We get along pretty well, but there are a few who think they're better than all of us. Marcia Mae, Paulie and Sam. They're jerks! The guys always 'accidentally' bump me with their shoulders and send my books flying, then they say they're sorry in a sarcastic way and walk away laughing. Marcia Mae's always telling me how big my ears are and that I smell funny. And they all do so many more things every day. I'm sick of it. I can't take it anymore!"

A swift kick to the table leg emphasizes Tray's point. The youngest Scout yips and skitters to his favorite sawdust pile to snuggle down in a less volatile space. He lays his head on his front paws and watches us with concerned eyebrows fluttering until he drifts into a blissful puppy sleep.

I raise myself onto the bar stool and rest my good fist on my hip. My dad instinct is to use that fist against the fathers who don't seem to be interested in raising kind children. I focus on my son's original question instead of the reason for it.

"Two fellows come to mind who might have a word about your question. Mr. Henry told Trayvon about the Marines who greeted the Montford Pointers when they arrived on Guadalcanal. He said some nodded and welcomed them, but there was a whole bunch who didn't. Some glared at them with what he called a 'simmerin' hate,' and others expressed their feelings with words and actions."

I watch my son's face and recognize the development of a case of righteous indignation in his red cheeks and furrowed brows.

"Mr. Henry told Trayvon how one guy approached them, a cigarette hanging out the corner of his mouth and a sneer holding it in place. 'Who let you people in those uniforms?' One of Mr. Henry's buddies—his name was Joe—stood straighter and answered, 'We earned 'em.'

"That fellow let out some words Mama'd wash my mouth out with soap for repeating and told them, 'Y'all haven't earned nuthin' and you ain't worthy of that emblem. Y'all don't let me catch you anywhere near me.' I remember Trayvon shaking as he recalled those words his grandpa'd shared with him. I asked him what his grandpa did. He said he grabbed hold of his buddy Joe to keep him from waging his own war right then and there against the man."

"I would've been on Joe's side! Mr. Henry should've let him go."

"Honestly, I probably would've felt the same way. Mr. Henry was a wiser man than us, though. He knew anger and fighting don't fix anything. Hate, pride and jealousy are three of the strongest—and deadliest—emotions. He didn't want Joe to get beat by them.

"Other guys hassled the Montford Pointers. They called them all the names they could think of and tripped them on their way back from getting their daily food rations. Others mocked them and said things like, 'Y'all leave them fellas alone. They got strong backs to carry stuff. That's why they're here, after all. Somebody's gotta make sure we don't run out of bullets up there on the front lines. Y'all boys think you can handle that?' Trayvon asked his grandpa why he didn't shoot them right there."

My son punches his palm with a fist and says, "I'd have asked the same thing!"

"My friend said his grandpa chuckled and shook his head. 'Now, Trayvon, Jesus called us to turn the other cheek. So, that's what I did—many times a day. I was feelin' a bit whiplashed, but I knew God had plans for us bein' there— bigger ones than causin' a ruckus over a bunch of fellas too ignorant to recognize fellow Marines when they met 'em.'

"And so, honorary chaplain Pop preached to them every day to hold their heads high, keep their tongues in check and reserve their anger for the mutual enemy they'd all face when they hit the beach on Guam. He coached them to look out for each other and stick together. Practical jokes and mean pranks didn't work so well when they gave each other a warning or helping hand. 'Two pairs of eyes are better than one, and a friend keeps his buddy's balance,' he told Trayvon."

I notice the tension and tightness of anger fading in my son's body language. If I share these stories right, he might learn more than one lesson; so, like I do multiple times during every serious conversation with the son God entrusted to me, I pray for wisdom.

"Early on July 26, 1944, the Japanese hit our Marines with non-stop attacks. There wasn't a moment to breathe; the fight kept coming. Mr. Henry told Trayvon the ground was slippery from the blood shed on both sides. On one of their return trips from re-supplying the front lines, he and his friend Joe—the one who'd faced the bully on their first day—heard a weak cry for help. They dodged and ducked a bullet barrage until they reached the man who'd spoken hateful words to them a few months before.

"Mr. Henry said Joe's jaw tensed. Joe had no desire to help the man who hated him and every Marine who looked like him. If they didn't carry him back to the medics, though, the man would die.

"Joe looked at Trayvon's grandpa and said, 'Pop, I don't want to do this.' Mr. Henry looked him in the eyes and asked, 'Are you going to?' 'If you're gonna look at me like that, then I suppose I've got to. Let's get him and get the heck outta here before we all get killed.' Their choice saved the man's life.

"As the heroes turned to load up with ammo and return to the firefight, the man grabbed Joe's ankle. Joe dropped to a knee beside the once hate-filled man and heard the whispered words, 'Thank you, Marine. I'm sorry.' Mr. Henry said he'd never seen such a genuine apology in his life. The man passed out then, but he was in the medic's care. As Mr. Henry and Joe carried another load back, Trayvon's grandpa noticed some moisture in his friend's eyes when he turned to say, 'Hope he'll make it. Maybe what we're doin' here will win more than one fight.'"

My son's busy arranging boards I'd stacked up for him to practice drilling holes. He remains quiet for a few moments.

"You said there were two fellows who came to mind?"

"I sure did. The other's Jesus. He lived a sinless life, always healing, teaching, loving, setting straight. They killed Him like they would have a murderer. Up on that cross, in all that pain—agony caused by the sins He willingly took from us because we couldn't save ourselves—He looked up to heaven and said three powerful words, 'Father, forgive them.' Makes you think, doesn't it?"

"Yeah." Tray's head lowers. "I think what Trayvon's grandpa said is something I should tell the other kids in my class who are sick of the bullies, too. The thing about 'Two eyes ...'—what was that again?"

"'Two pairs of eyes are better than one, and a friend keeps his buddy's balance.'"

Tray dashes to my desk and returns with a notepad and pen, his faithful canine companion chasing after him and spreading sawdust along the way.

"Say it one more time? I want to write it down."

I smile and thank God for giving my son understanding beyond his years. "You got it, bud."

§

Late 2026: 12 years old, sixth grade

"What do Marines and soldiers do when there's not a war?"

I can tell the past fifteen minutes of practice with the hand saw is getting to Tray. It'll take him a while to get used to the new skill, and I mentally scold myself for forgetting to have him put on gloves before today's lesson.

"Hey bud, let me make sure you're not getting blisters." I check his hand and discover an angry red spot forming at the base of his thumb. Scout Three sits next to us at attention, his furry eyebrows dancing out his concern.

While I search through my first aid kit, I acknowledge Tray's question. "Before we shipped out, we did a lot of training—shooting, drills, PT—and a ton of marching. Marines' marching is what civilians would call running, by the way."

My son's responding chuckle to the corny joke I know he's heard before satisfies me, and I smile as I bandage him up. When I'm done, Scout nuzzles Tray for ear rubs and gets his wish.

"We also learned what jobs we might be good at. The officers determined what part of the Corps we'd be most helpful in, and we attended special schools. Some guys were good at working on machines and engines. They'd go to places like the air wing, where they'd work on our helicopters."

"Your job was to shoot, right?"

"Yes, sir! Trayvon's, too. We were extra good at it; that's why we both got chosen for Scout Sniper School."

"What would have happened if there hadn't been a war for y'all to go to?"

I push away the "what if" answers that flood my mind and choose not to focus on the pictures of a right arm that isn't gimpy or a best friend who isn't dead.

"Well, I can't know the answer to that for sure. Maybe to better answer your question, I'll tell you about another friend of mine. Have I ever mentioned Daryl?" Tray shakes his head and sits beside Scout for another "warrior tale," as he calls the stories I share with him. "Daryl Jenkins was one of my friends at Harvey's shooting range."

"Harvey fought in Vietnam, right?" I nod; then he asks, "Was Daryl a Marine too?"

"He was an Army Ranger—a soldier with extra training to carry out special missions during wartime ... and outside of wartime. His unit was in Saudi Arabia in 1991 while our country was involved in the war Operation Desert Storm.

Daryl didn't talk a whole lot about what he did while he served, but I do know two big missions he was part of outside of wartime: Operation Just Cause and Operation Gothic Serpent. That last one led to a rough and unexpected battle."

Tray and Scout perk up and I know I've got their attention. It's the cool names.

"The first op involved entering a country called Panama at the end of 1989 to arrest a dictator who'd done a lot of bad things, like hurting innocent people and threatening the safety of Americans who lived there. The Rangers did their job quickly and well."

"What war was that?"

"Well, that's the thing. Just because our country isn't at war doesn't mean our world's at peace. That's where guys like Daryl come in. If Americans away from home are threatened or other countries don't have their own guardian warriors, we share ours."

"I didn't know we did that."

"Sure enough! Now, the second op in 1993 was way more complicated. The United States sent troops to Somalia the year before to provide help to a country that was starving. A bunch of warlords had caused a civil war there and didn't want other countries coming in to help the people they'd hurt. One of the worst of those leaders had sent soldiers to kill people who were distributing food and medicine.

"That's when they sent some of our military, including Daryl and other Rangers, to arrest the warlord and his top leaders. Instead of it being an in-and-out mission, though, two of our helicopters got shot down. Daryl's two best friends were killed, and his unit endured what's been called the most intense groundfight since Vietnam."

The tragedy constricts my lungs as I listen to my heartbeat, deafening in the silence. I remember how it sounded when Trayvon's heart stopped and imagine how much harder it would have been if I'd had to witness what Daryl did: his friends' bodies dragged around the streets of a foreign nation they thought they were there to help through a quick mission, while the rest of their unit was trapped by guerrilla soldiers. He must have wondered if he'd ever make it home from that one. Daryl had reasons for staying quiet when the other guys swapped stories at the range.

Scout's whimper draws me back to the present in my woodshop, and I grin at the dog's twitching eyebrows. He's definitely a worrywart. I squat and scratch behind his ear while Tray rubs his chin. Our double-team eases his anxiety, and Scout lays in Tray's lap to listen to the rest of our discussion.

"My friend Colton told me one day that he always worries about his dad when he gets deployed, even though we're not at war. Now I understand why. Maybe I shouldn't just tell him his dad will be fine."

"Kind words are always nice to share with friends. Another important action is to listen to his worries and fears. It's good to have people you can talk to about anything."

"That's why I'm glad you and me talk in here every day. I know if there's ever anything that scares or worries me, I can tell you."

"I'm glad you know that, bud. I'm always here for you." After a shoulder bump, I ask, "Think you can finish that last cut with your saw?"

"You bet!"

Scout pops up at Tray's shout and sprints with his buddy across the shop. "I better grab my gloves first."

"Good call! That might keep us out of trouble with Mama."

"I won't be in trouble. You, on the other hand, ..."

"Watch it there!" I rub my knuckle on the top of his head as he slips on gloves. Scout's eyebrows commence another worry flutter, and Tray and I shake our heads at the wolfhound's concern.

§

Late 2027: 13 years old, seventh grade

I ate too much again. My stomach might pop. Perhaps I've reached the age where I should stop before I reach thirds or fourths … even if it is Thanksgiving. I set down the horse I've been whittling and rub my belly again as I observe Tray's progress on his duck.

He's getting better every day, and I'm amazed again at his natural talent. I wish Senior could see him. The old man's bushy eyebrows would dance all over his forehead if he saw my son work.

I envision an anxious Scout Three and an excited Senior and wonder whose eyebrows would dance more.

"What's so funny?"

My son's question surprises me until I realize I laughed out loud. "I was thinking how much Senior would love to watch you work. He was a great teacher. I believe he'd be impressed with how quickly you've taken to whittling."

"I'm glad he taught you so you could teach me."

When I pick up my work again, I search for ways to improve the back leg that's giving me trouble.

"Dad?"

"Mmm-hmmm?"

"How can we be grateful in a world full of so much bad? I know we're supposed to give thanks every day and all that, but … well … things sometimes feel hopeless."

I consider his question and how I've asked the same one in multiple forms over the years.

"Are you thinking about last week's school shooting?"

He nods. "I can't stop thinking about it. I mean, most of those kids were my age. They were probably looking forward to their Thanksgiving break, just like me."

"When I was a kid, we had a bunch of school shootings around the country. Every time, the tragedy hit us hard, and we felt a dark cloud of gloom over our hallways. It was scary."

I remember the shootings that had, in some ways, defined my generation and how the attacks on 9/11 felt like the next step in increasing violence that became part of life. Of course, our daily violence doesn't hold a candle to what kids in many countries grow up surrounded by—if they grow up at all.

"Evil exists. It's everywhere and consumes everything. The truth is, though, we serve a God who's greater than evil. In fact, He's already defeated it, so we can give thanks and find ways to shine God's good light, despite the darkness. We can share smiles with people who are hurting and show them God's love."

Tray smooths out the duck's back before he says, "I don't know, Dad. Some evil feels too dark to smile through. Like the world wars—almost the whole world killing each other—how did anyone share God's love then?"

"I've told you before about Mr. Henry. He didn't just shine; he lit up those islands. Trayvon told me how his grandfather prayed with and for many Marines and soldiers as they breathed their last. He was a peacemaker. He exemplified how to be a friend and love all neighbors, and he led many folks to Christ—all during war."

"How'd you learn to do that?" I don't hide my amazement as I examine the feathers my son is carving into his duck.

"Well, Dad, I have been watching you work for thirteen years. Besides, it makes sense when you think about the animal you're carving and look closely at the wood you're holding."

I chuckle at my son's confidence and natural ability. He'll be taking over the shop before long. Retirement doesn't sound half bad. I can almost hear Senior's "Humph!" He wasn't a fan of "the R word," as he called it.

"You know, your learning by watching me reminds me of something that happened to Senior. He told me he was embarrassed of his thoughts at the beginning of the war. When they headed west, he loathed the Japanese for what they'd done to our country. Once they began fighting, he allowed hatred to take over. He took pleasure in ending their lives because he let rage fester into malice.

"Often during the battles to take each island, Marines and soldiers faced stealthy surprise attacks or sudden Banzai attacks—where Japanese soldiers screamed while rushing into Americans' trenches, bayonets outstretched. Our men never knew when the enemy might strike, so they endured many sleepless nights."

I focus on the final hoof of the horse in my hand before I set the finished product to the side and continue Senior's story.

"One night, on what felt like the dark side of the eternity he spent atop Bloody Ridge, Senior was whisper-cursing the Japanese soldiers when one of his buddies, a man named Hank, grabbed his vest and pulled him close. 'They're men, same as us; made by the same God, in the same image. We're all human beings, all fighting for the folks we love, all hoping to make it to the dawn. Give them names if you need to, but don't let your hate destroy that heart of yours.'

"Senior sneered at his friend's preaching and sarcastically replied, 'You gonna feel the same way when one of them's bayonets finds your heart?' 'I do.' Senior said those were Hank's last words. His friend had been stabbed. Hank knew he wouldn't make it, so he used his final breaths to urge Senior to be a better man and view even enemies with love and compassion.

"From then on, Senior fought just as hard, but he saw the Japanese soldiers for who they were—guys the same age as him, perhaps with pregnant wives of their own back home who carried the sons they hoped to meet. Whenever Senior heard others echoing his words of hate, he'd share Hank's words and example ... even when he, too, was seriously wounded soon after his friend's death. Many of the Marines around him also viewed their enemies with more compassion as the war continued, and Senior credited that Christlike attitude with keeping their souls intact when they returned home.

"He said by the time they won the Battle of Okinawa, he longed for an end to the killing and a beginning of restoration to that devastated land. As he witnessed young Japanese soldiers launching themselves off what came to be called the 'Suicide Cliffs,' he hit his knees and wept. He told me he felt no victory after watching the hopelessness in the eyes of those men."

The duck rests in Tray's palm as Senior's experience settles into his heart.

"Senior joined a host of Marines who moved onto Japan's mainland. He had promised the men who'd taken their own lives—and the ones whose lives he'd taken—that he would show love and kindness to all the Japanese citizens he met. That's a promise he kept with every little animal or flower he whittled out of whatever pieces of bomb-charred wood he could find."

I pick up Tray's duck and examine his handiwork before handing it back for him to add more details to the feathers. Watching my son's careful knife skills, I wonder what it must have been like for Senior to walk through the aftermath of the bomb on Nagasaki. Thousands of innocent people died there and in Hiroshima. I imagine the children, the families—all whose lives changed forever on those days.

Tray sets his tools aside and runs his fingers across the work he's done. "This year was the eighty-second anniversary of the bombings. Our class watched videos about them and read books, too—nonfiction and fiction ones based on that time. The bombings were awful. Dad, do you think there will ever be another atomic bomb used?"

"I pray not."

"Maybe adults like you can keep that from happening until my friends and I can take over."

I nod a smile at my son. I hoist myself up and approach my wall of hand tools. Many of them belonged to Senior. I reach to where two nails hold up something Senior made many years ago.

"When Senior told me what I've shared with you today, he showed me this. It hung in his shop, but I'd never asked him about it."

Tray holds out his hand, and I place a blackened piece of wood in his palm.

"Senior had led me to his workshop to recover and breathe. I hadn't been off the mountain long, and it was my first visit to Columbia in five years. Mawmaw Mabel had invited the entire Miller clan and many church friends to welcome me back and celebrate that I'd accepted Christ as my Savior. That many people crowded in the house overwhelmed me. Senior recognized my panic and ushered me out back to his shop."

I give thanks that Senior understood my post-war anxiety. He'd marched in the same boots, after all. He also understood the guilt I held, so he gave me this reminder. One day I'll pass it on to Tray.

"Senior gave me this as a reminder that beauty can still bloom after darkness."

I watch Tray reverently rub the black wooden cherry blossom and know he understands its significance as I share my thoughts.

"We will keep the tragedies of Hiroshima and Nagasaki from happening again by never forgetting the people who died. We also remember that even in the devastation and blackness of two atomic bombs, love and light couldn't be destroyed. Senior didn't lose his soul through the hell of war. Instead, he discovered a way to share hope through these small gifts he made and the simple phrase he always said as he gave them to the children he met: 'God loves you, and so do I.'"

§

Late 2028: 14 years old, eighth grade

"You've been quiet this week. Everything okay?"

My son sands slower than usual as he smooths his latest decorative outline. We began lessons on the scroll saw a few weeks ago, and he's taken to the challenge as well as everything I've taught him.

"Yeah." His tone doesn't convince me any more than his half-hearted sanding, a task he typically tackles with gusto.

I reach over and tap his wrist. "I can tell it's not. Spit it out."

He sighs as he sets the wood next to the saw. "I'm realizing how much tougher everything in life is getting. Algebra, football playoffs ... even the shop."

As he points to the power saw, I reflect on my poor response to the days my son's fast approaching. I thought falling into a bottle would make everything about growing up easier ... or make me care less that I wasn't up to the new challenges in my life—like the loss of several friends my freshman year. I snap my focus back on Tray and his concerns.

"I hate to tell you, that's how life goes. Every task gets tougher, but as they do, you'll rise to meet them. Plus, you've got guides for your journey. For school, you've got teachers and coaches. For life in general, you've got your mama and me, Nana and Grandpa. We're all here for you, and we've been where you are. You're not alone in this life."

Tray picks at the sandpaper in his hand. I sense a deeper question coming and wait for him to release it. He walks to the fridge for drinks, and I turn my attention and hands to Scout Three.

The dog grins his appreciation for my petting and thumps his back paw on the floor when I reach the special spot behind his ear.

Tray speaks as he crosses to our side of the shop.

"The truth is, I start high school next year, which feels too soon. Life feels like it's hit fast-forward—like I'm going to blink and it'll be graduation and then college, a career … the 'real world.' It's just too dang fast."

He offers me a sports drink as he sits beside me. I accept it, much to Scout's chagrin at losing his massage. "Try being a few sleeps away from half a century."

Tray chokes on his drink, and I slap his back a few times.

"It's not that funny, you know."

He soothes our concerned dog and laughs at my sarcasm. "Don't worry, Dad. You've got a few more years before we check you into the old folks' home."

I punch his arm before he continues.

"In all seriousness, everything I'm learning now feels really, really important. Like, if I miss something in the next few years, I'm going to be screwed the rest of my life."

As I nod and take a few more sips, I ponder my response. I was such a train wreck at his age and at the start of my adult life. He'd do better talking to Rachael than me. I set down my drink and resume Scout's face massage. The motion calms me as much as the dog. It also helps me focus.

"I can tell you what it was like as a young adult training for war. We were all scared out of our minds. They had trained us at the highest caliber, no doubt; but we still wondered as we headed into that godforsaken desert if it was anywhere near enough. Would we remember our training? Would we be there for our buddies when it mattered? Would we freeze up?"

My jaws clench—hard—and I focus on the pain and on the motion of rubbing behind Scout's ears. I mentally remind myself not to fixate on my mistakes. At the end of the day, my training was enough. I was as ready as any human could possibly be to face an enemy whose life I was expected to take before he took mine—or the guy's next to me.

"The point I want to make is every person—no matter what they do with their life or what training they have to do it—will make mistakes. Many of them. It's through mistakes we often learn the greatest lessons."

Tray chugs the rest of his drink. He screws on the cap and sets up the bottle to soar across tables and saws toward the trash can. After landing the impressive shot, Tray asks, "What if I do miss something vital? Like, a life lesson just doesn't stick?"

"If that happens, I believe you'll realize you're missing a piece to the puzzle. In Iraq, there were tactics or details specific to the terrain or enemy that our instructors didn't know to teach us, even in Urban Sniper training. When we arrived in country, the guys we replaced filled us in on all the things they knew we hadn't been taught back home—things many of them had learned in the hardest of ways."

I give Scout one more scratch under his chin before I stand and squeeze Tray's shoulder.

"What specifically is tough about the things you mentioned earlier?"

"Well, algebra's got letters in it. That's just weird."

"Can't argue with you there, man."

"Football … well, I guess it's not harder. It's just … the wins and losses mean more when everyone's counting on a championship victory. All anyone at school ever talks to me about is how I feel about the next game and how tough our opponent will be. I get to a point where I want to scream at them that I can't tell the future."

I smile at the validity to his frustration. "People focus on the least important things at times. I think it's how they deal with whatever bigger issues they're facing."

"That makes sense." Tray returns to his decorative pieces and scrutinizes them. He rubs sandpaper around a rough corner. "Honestly, this isn't harder either, and I like using more of the cool tools in here."

"Cool tools come with maturity, responsibility and practice." I wink and smile.

Tray shakes his head at my line, then addresses the heart of his concerns. "I think it's just that, a lot of times, when I hit a harder task, I want to go back to my first hammer and toolbelt and end the day with Mama reading me a story. If that makes sense."

"Makes perfect sense to me, man. I can't begin to number how many times over the years I've felt the same way. When I was a kid, all I wanted was to be an adult so I could do whatever I wanted."

Tray laughs. "All I wanted was to get old enough to use the cool tools!"

"Exactly! With good aspects to a new stage of life come the three things I mentioned: maturity, responsibility and practice. You're always going to face times when you want to quit. I do. Ask your mama, Nana and Grandpa. I guarantee, they do, too. Surround yourself with strong people—friends who have similar goals to yours, good leaders, role models, mentors. They will be there to advise, encourage and support you as you grow."

"So, I need to get used to challenges and suck it up, right?"

I feel his eyes rolling, even if I can't see them. "How about I share something Senior told me when he drove me to the bus for Boot Camp?"

Tray sets down his work, and I have his full attention.

"Senior said when they were fighting for every inch on Bloody Ridge, he wanted more than anything to throw down his weapon, turn around and walk—if he had to—all the way to his wife and son-on-the-way.

"Instead of feeling sorry for himself, he started saying, 'I won't give up—not before this next step.' Every time he'd take a step—forward or backward—he'd say that. He said as he did, he became more focused. The Japanese soldiers finally retreated, and our guys took the Ridge. He repeated that mantra, one step at a time, all the way to the war's end … three long years later."

"'I won't give up—not before this next step.'" My son repeats Senior's words, and I thank God for the smile spreading across his face. "I'll remember that. Thanks, Dad; and thanks for being here for me. I know I can turn to you if I don't know what to do or discover I'm missing a skill."

"You sure can. Now, how about you clean up this mess and let's see what Mama and Nana are rustling up in the kitchen? Carolina said dinner will end with something chocolatey."

"I'm not giving up before that step!"

§

Late 2029: 14 years old, ninth grade

Tray unplugs the jigsaw he used to cut out a coffee tabletop for my mom. I lean forward in my seat to rub Scout Three's face. He's no fan of the noisier tools, so I came to sit with him once I finished staining a fresh batch of picture frames. My notoriously anxious dog calms beneath my hands, and I swear he smiles.

I watch Tray examine his work with a craftsman's critical eye. He's been unusually quiet today. Actually, his mood drastically shifted last night after he talked with his buddy Henry. My dessert-loving son even declined a second bowl of ice cream.

Tray packs away the jigsaw and tosses his safety goggles and gloves in a bag for the next day's shop class—a course he and I petitioned our high school to add to their curriculum. As Tray crosses the shop to sit with us, I notice the stoop in his shoulders and shadows in his eyes.

"I'm worried about you son. You haven't looked right since you talked with Henry last night. What's going on?"

"Dad, I don't know what to do." Tray buries his face in his hands for a moment, then runs his hands through his hair before straightening. "Henry asked me not to tell anyone, but I can't do that."

I give my son time and space to work out what he needs to share. His inner angst shows in the red of his cheeks and in his eyes. While I wait for him to elaborate, I realize we're entering a deeper stage of communication and pray for wisdom and right words.

"Henry said he wants to kill himself." Tray's words are barely a whisper. In the shrug of his shoulders and tremble of his lip, I can see verbalizing the facts doesn't bring any more sense than they held in his mind. "I don't know what to do with that."

Tray rubs his eyes before continuing. "I didn't sleep at all last night. I was so worried he'd do something. Then, this morning, I didn't hear from him, so I went by his house. He said the same stuff again. He doesn't want me to tell anyone, and he didn't want me to leave. I told him he could come with me, but that I had work to do here today. He really made it feel like if I left him, he was going to do something. I can't always be with him, and I don't know how to help him. What do I do, Dad?"

My heart sinks as I feel the weight of the burden my son carries. I know the heaviness of feeling responsibility for someone's life. I also know where Henry is. I'd been that hopeless, lost and desperate multiple times.

I wonder if now is the time to share my past struggles with my son. My mind flashes back to the times I believed ending it all was the only choice before me, and I think about why I'm still here.

"First, you don't need to carry this burden alone and neither does Henry. Don't think for one second that you are ultimately responsible for his actions or emotions. Yes, he came to you, which means he must trust you. Your telling me is not a breach of that trust, though. You are correct that this isn't something either of you should handle on your own. It's too huge."

I take a deep breath to prepare for the second part of my answer. As Tray gets older, I need to face unpleasant aspects of my past so he and his friends can avoid the mistakes I made.

"Second, I've been where Henry is … more than once. I came close to stepping on a track ahead of a barreling freight train, and I held a gun in my hands with the intent to end it all."

Tray doesn't look stunned, like I thought he would. He leans forward and nods his head.

"I know the war was tough on you, and I know you go to meetings with the other veterans. I mean, I didn't know you'd almost killed yourself, but it makes sense. Honestly, I wish I would have thought about that last night because Henry might have talked to you."

"Well, I'm here now. Give Henry a call. Tell him that you told me; tell him what I said and that I want to help him. Tell him I want to talk with him and his parents. He's going to need their support, and I know they want to give him that. Ask him if he'd rather come here or have us there."

While Tray calls his friend, I busy around the shop, picking up scraps and shavings from my classes that day. I return stain cans to their proper shelves and spread out the rags on a rack I made for that purpose. Over the years, its wood has soaked in every stain I've ever used.

I think of the many lessons I've learned—from my own experiences and from the advice of wiser people in my life. Like stain, those lessons seeped into my life and colored my actions and decisions. Now, I can impress them upon a new generation.

As I hang the final rag, Tray approaches. His step is lighter and his posture straighter.

"Henry took what I told him well—didn't get upset or hang up on me. He told me he realized after I left this morning that he needs more help, but he wasn't sure how to get it. I told him everything you said, and he is going to talk to his parents right now. They'll call us in a little while. I'm glad I told you; I felt so helpless and kept thinking I should have done more last night."

"You did two very important things—you listened to him, and you told me. Those are the two things you needed to do. There is a third thing."

"If you're going to say prayer, I did that all night."

"That's the trifecta!"

Tray's smile lightens my heart, until I watch the concern roll across his face and settle in a crease between his eyebrows.

"Dad, is Henry going to be okay?"

His look reminds me of the time he swallowed his tooth and came to me for reassurance. The stakes and consequences are far higher now than they were then.

"Well, son, I pray he will. We are going to surround him with the support he needs, but, at the end of the day, Henry has some big choices to make. He can accept help, or he can refuse. He can try to cope on his own. I chose wrong for many years, and I will always regret that. Like everything else in the past, I can't change my choice. What I can do is learn from it and use it. Today, I'm going to use it to reach out to Henry."

Tray's eyes shift from fearful to determined as we carefully slide the drop cloth holding the drying frames closer to the wall. My son squats to examine each frame, testing a few places for dryness. I can tell he's picturing how I achieved the designs in the wood and probably thinking of how he could improve on them. He's beginning to rival my skill level with such details.

After a minute of silence, Tray asks, "What changed things for you?"

"Community."

My answer surprises us both with its simplicity and quickness. I think back to all the people in my life who have walked beside me, encouraged me, spoken truth to me, prayed for me and refused to let me succumb to the darkness within.

"For too many years after losing Trayvon and leaving the Corps, I tried to do things on my own. Of course, that was the worst idea. But, even when I came to Grandpa and understood

God's grace and mercy, I missed the importance of community in my struggles. I thought being a Christian would make everything magically better, but the nightmares and doubts and misbeliefs still clouded my heart.

"Grandpa and Nana and Mama were there for me, but I needed more help—counseling, discipleship, accountability. I also had to learn to recognize when my mind was turning against me so I could reach out to my community.

"Too many times, I tried to repress my emotions and fears instead of sharing them with the people who wanted to help me process them."

Tray's slow nod shows he's sifting my response for golden nuggets to enrich his friendship with Henry.

"Community. Yeah, that makes sense. Henry's going to need that now. I can be part of that for him. It's still scary, but not nearly as much as it was when I was all he had. I've never felt that useless."

"Honestly, one of the greatest things about being a Christian is we never need to be alone. We are surrounded by others who trust Christ, follow His commands and commit to help one another. With their support and God's word guiding us, we can grow and mature faster than we ever could alone."

"Thanks for sharing part of your story with me and for sharing it with Henry, too. I'm sorry you went through all the bad stuff you did, but I'm thankful you can help us now."

"Me too, bud. Me too."

As he stands, nearly as tall as me, I make a decision. I was going to wait another year to teach him to use the table saw, but maybe he is ready after all.

"While we wait to hear from Henry, I'm going to teach you to use the table saw."

Tray whoops, and Scout whimpers as he lays flat, head resting on his front paws. The dog's eyebrows commence their worry dance. He much prefers quieter, less dangerous tools.

"Now, don't get too excited. Today we begin safety training."

Scout's eyebrows slow as he raises his head, crosses his paws and pants lazily. No one will ever convince me dogs don't understand every word we say.

Tray's love of power tools is matched in intensity by a loathing for my slow-and-steady approach to teaching him to use them.

"'Today we start' means I might get to touch it before I'm twenty."

"Not with that attitude."

Scout's bark registers his agreement with me.

Legacy of Healing

"Of His own will He brought us forth by
the word of truth, that we might be a kind
of firstfruits of His creatures."
James 1:18

Joy of Forgiveness

I can't watch them drive away.

Even without a sight line into the minivan as it weaves along the dogwood-lined drive, I envision my husband's solemn expression. Worry and a hint of fear flickered around the edges of his eyes during our goodbyes as he evaluated our four little ones—no doubt contemplating the monumental challenge of keeping them all fed, clothed and semi-clean.

The memorized images of each child's face threaten to unhinge my resolve to take this next step—to move on from the mountainous physical recovery, through the valleys of emotional and spiritual healing.

Guilt, pain, loss, fear. One warring emotion jostles the next as they vibrate to my erratic internal beat. I fear the elastic in my chest will snap with any greater expansion of my heart and contemplate chasing the retreating vehicle.

Instead, I picture my family's faces once more and move forward for them, for us. I squeeze the lever on the handle before me and enter a cheerful hallway—sunny yellow with patches of twinkling tulips and promising primroses—so bright I blink when I slide off my sunglasses. These walls contrast the lifeless tones of the hospital where my body was purged from the poison on which I depended. The hope-laden wall whispers verses as I pass.

*"Jesus Christ is the same yesterday, today
and forever." - Hebrews 13:8*

*"Therefore, if anyone is in Christ, he is a new
creation; old things have passed away; behold, all
things have become new." - II Corinthians 5:17*

The verse repeats as an inner prayer with each footstep.

All Things ...

New ....

One tan leather strap slips from my shoulder; I tuck it under its partner as I shift the overnight bag once more. I splash again in the shallows of the irony. I'll be here long past one night.

As I clutch the preppy sailor bag against my chest, I remember women's retreats. The worship, the Bible studies, the prayers—all punctuated by sips from the water bottle I carried and frequently refilled from the jar this overnight bag hid.

A familiar burning erupts in my throat—a physical clue that my guilt, shame and brokenness remains unquenchable. I swallow the flame, choke on its embers and clench my eyes against the smoke billowing across my family's past.

Become new ...

I open my eyes again at the entrance to my temporary home. A decorative silver 114 rests atop a hanging vase of fresh gerbera daisies. Their wistfulness winks at me as I swipe any emotional overflow from my cheeks.

Smile on. Chin up. Move forward.

The doorknob's icy jolt thrusts me into the present as I swing the door into an image I'll never forget.

The young girl sits cross-legged on the twin bed. Her blond hair cascades around her, and her gaze fixates far beyond the windowpanes. A sunbeam spotlights her, its illumination congregating on the tip of her chin and spilling upon the hands that hold up her world—a belly swollen with life.

She turns as I enter; our eyes lock.

Emotions splinter in the lighter blue flecks of her irises— uncertainty, pain, shame, hurt, brokenness. In the darker edges I glimpse something else. An emotion feeble as the spindly-legged fawn I watched in our backyard the day after I returned from the hospital.

Shaky but determined, hope rises on the young woman's face.

Through our wordless greeting, I return her fledgling feeling and decide, *We can do this. Together. With God.*

"Hi there! I'm Jaida."

My roommate's smile shimmers behind the clouds of uncertainty drifting across her face. "I'm Shannon." Her bare whisper reaches my ear, and my mother heart twinges.

God, guide me in loving this child of yours. Help me help her. Cast off my uselessness, fear and doubt. Bolster my faith in you. Use me.

"We have a beautiful view, don't we?" I ask, as the sunlight dancing on the pond glistens back at us. Shannon's clouds dissipate, revealing the radiance her smile can relay.

"It doesn't look real, does it? Like faeries dancing on the water."

We can do this. Together. With God.

The stretch of the smile on my face feels right. I've missed its unhindered, genuine feel. *Thank you for this spot of joy and for this young woman.*

"Pastor Ben's daughter, Rachael, told me they have chocolate pudding every night. Do you think they'll let me start with dessert?"

A laugh I thought I'd lost rustles past my ears. "I bet we could persuade them. After all, a girl needs her chocolate. I'll put my clothes away, and maybe we can walk to the cafeteria together?"

She nods acceptance of my request, slides awkwardly from her bed and opens the third dresser drawer for me.

"I used the top two. Is that okay?" Worry deepens creases a teen shouldn't bear. "It's hard to bend over these days."

"Sounds familiar! I've been at that stage four times now."

I lift shirts, skirts, shorts, pants, pajamas and underwear as we chat. Once everything spreads across the baby blue handmade quilt, I refold each item and fill the two bottom drawers. "Have you worn mismatched shoes out yet?"

A hint of childhood lightens Shannon's laugh. "I did a couple days ago. My dad took me for ice cream. We saw so many people I hadn't seen in years. It wasn't until we'd been there a while that I propped my feet on the booth across from me. There they were—one red tennis shoe, one pink. I started bawling, and it took my poor dad about fifteen minutes to figure out why."

Hilarity bubbles inside me as I picture the man's helplessness. "Men often find themselves at a loss when it comes to us women, especially when our hormones are surging."

I unpack my toiletry bag. Shampoo, conditioner, deodorant, brush, toothbrush, toothpaste—the necessities. No makeup. I'm done with masks, though I'm uncertain how to live bared to the world around me. I close the bottom drawer as Shannon slides her feet into sandals. Her smile is hesitant but open—to friendship and to a future where hope might still exist.

"Let's get some of that pudding!" We link arms. The motion of reaching out to another human sends a wave of thankfulness across me as Shannon laughs at my exclamation. We become allies in our pursuit of pudding and inner peace.

§

Back in the reality of our room, Shannon swings her shower caddy as she shuffles toward the bathroom. We trade smiles. Mine fades when she closes the door.

Is a smile always a mask? Will I ever feel genuine joy again?

Did I ever feel it?

The day I gave my life to Christ: I was young, but the certainty was more solid than anything I had felt before or have since. Thankfulness. Confidence. Joy.

Time with my best friends: Girls' weekends, nights out, nights in. Maisie, Leena, Sandy and I have ridden the rapids of abuse, adultery, miscarriages, job loss ... addiction. Pain and grief together, but oh so much joy. Sharing through everything—no ultimatums, regardless of distance or time—acceptance of who we are, how we are, how we're not. No perfection expected; masks at the door. Always.

Almost always. When did I start lying to them?

When did I start lying to myself?

Our wedding: The white dress with the cathedral train. It was the dream, until life swept it away. Somewhere along the way, he stopped listening, seeing, feeling. So did I.

Who stopped first?

Does it matter?

My babies' births: Only true joy could overshadow the pain of thirty-two hours of labor, times four. Forty tiny fingers; forty curled toes. Four crinkled noses; four trusting hearts.

Joy: I once held it, gave it, shared it, lived it.

How do I shift from where I am now—mask-less, guilty, pain-filled, uncertain but hope ... not full ... perhaps hope-sprinkled?—to where I'd like to be, still mask-less, but also painless, sure and steady? Joy-filled and hopeful?

The door reopens. Shannon, hair damp and skin shower-reddened, emerges. Smiles flash again. Her shower gel fragrance drifts on the closing door's breeze, carrying the innocence and softness of flower petals and memories of spring picnics in a meadow beneath cotton ball skies.

Mask-less, our smiles convey honesty. They don't cover mistakes or heartbreak. They widen, despite those things. They are a choice. A choice to move toward brighter futures, filled with joy.

Can I choose it?

§

I like Rose immediately. Honesty deepens the warm syrup shade of her eyes, and truth and grace drip from her lips as we begin our first counseling session.

We sit face to face, and I'm thankful she hasn't put her desk between us. This feels more intentional, inviting.

"Jaida, welcome! I'm eager to begin our time together to help you run toward a positive life full of all the hope and grace God shines on us."

My skeptical grin earns an addition to her greeting. "Not every day will be peaches and cream. God carries us through the cottage cheese and whole grain days, too."

Now, that's a genuine smile, I think, as my mouth, mind, heart and soul open to the woman before me. No masks. She exudes truth.

"Thank you."

The tear falls, and I let it as we inch closer, knees together. Deep breath, and I reveal my heart to this recent stranger.

"I became invisible. To my husband; to others. Most of all, to myself. I became who I thought others expected me to be. I rolled pretty paper across the walls I built. Layer by layer, I forgot the original intent of who I desired to be, how I longed to be—was created to be. The wallpaper weighed me down, and I longed to feel lighter."

Rose's eyes reveal empathy, so I continue unwrapping my burden. "Vodka wasn't too expensive. No color or smell. I never really liked the taste, but the feel ... or the lack ...."

My jagged laugh snags the scars of guilt and shame, and now I bleed.

"I never knew a person could be so exhausted. Many nights, I was too tired to sleep during my allotted five hours. Of course, most nights the kids took turns being up for three of those five—at least."

Next, I unearth a hidden truth I haven't yet spoken out loud.

"I hated every second of the life I called a blessing and had thought I wanted. I turned to a substance instead of doing the two things I should have—first, honestly communicate with the husband who didn't see or hear me because I never asked him to or showed him how and, second, fall at the feet of my heavenly Father who promises strength and peace. Instead, I added layers of cheery wallpaper I thought others wanted to see onto the eroding walls of my heart."

The room's light shifts. I envision the clouds outside the closed blinds drifting along on their journey to somewhere, bowing to the sun's brilliance in their passing.

"And now? How do you view this life of yours?"

Time ticks around us. I lift her question, turn it over, feel it in my mind. My words disturb my heart's soil, like weeds scattering earth in my herb garden.

"Part of me wants to run away. From my husband and his needs, his demands—many I fabricated. From the gossip and judging looks in our church. From my children ... my babies, with their incessant demands, needs, desires. The continual giving, pouring out, handing over."

Rose presses the tissue in my hand, but I let my emotions fall where they may as I blurt out a sob and an admission. "I've got nothing left to give."

Silence allows relief, reflection, release. Rose's words rise slowly, quietly … authoritatively.

"You cannot pour out what you don't contain. You've already acknowledged from where—from Whom—our strength comes, so you know where to run with your emptiness. Pressing forward requires you to turn knowledge into action as you daily remind yourself of your need for fuel—the right fuel."

"Not vodka fuel, huh?" Shame edges my joke.

In Rose's smile, I recognize an understanding of my heart, even with its dark spots. She identifies one with her next question.

"Do you crave it?"

Eyes connect. Truth. No mask. Emotions and heart bare.

"I crave the release, the removal of pain, the loss of the burden."

"And the vodka brought you those?"

Honesty lifts one corner of my mouth, even as I feel the phantom burn of the drink on my tongue, its quenching fire coating my throat. Deeper honesty raises the reminder of the bile it brought up—the foulness of my soul—especially on that final day under its control.

"Temporarily."

A nod, tight-lipped acknowledgment and more verity: "You crave permanent release, removal of pain and relief from the burdens."

I affirm her stated question. "I know the permanence comes from God alone. But how? In life's daily dregs, how can His freedom be lasting?"

"God doesn't promise ease; He promises His presence. In the darkness, in the overwhelm—in your lack—open your eyes to His light, His relief, His plenty. And while these intangibles are no less real, we can also clutch His presence in our hands."

I hadn't seen her pick it up, but I feel the gift she places in my hands. The smooth coolness of the leather cover slides into my palms, and I know, without looking down, the calming words contained in the pure white binding I cradle.

"The Psalms contain comfort, peace—reminders of all I know you both believe and crave. Let's begin there."

I nod to the Bible in my lap. Though I still feel their threat, the tears have dried; their flow dammed ... for now. "I'd like that" trickles over the spread of my lips as Rose returns my wishful smile with a hope-filled one.

"Tonight and tomorrow morning, read one, part of one or fifty. Pray for God's guidance in the number and clarity in your understanding. Write down your questions, reflections and any truths you unearth in this rich mine."

Her hand clutches mine as we bow heads before our heavenly father. "God, we ask right now for a shift in Jaida's cravings. Move her to crave the sweet drops of your word, of time in your presence, of the filling permanence of your peace."

We end our first session with a duet: "In Jesus' name, amen."

That close begins my future, and I know God will use Rose to guide me on the right onward path.

§

"I'm Jaida Masters. I'm a preacher's wife and mom to four precious kiddos." I nod to Pastor Burns and look around the circle.

Next to me, Shannon rubs the marks on her arm, a habit I recognize as her coping with nerves. Across from me, another teen—weighed down more than a child should be—fixes his eyes on the toes of his sneakers. I sense the fear he tries to hide. On the other side of me, an older gentleman radiates kindness, but I feel the vice grip a mixture of sorrow and shame presses into him. I clutch to my chest the Bible Rose gave me. Its solidity emboldens me to continue. "I'm also a recovering alcoholic."

I rest the Bible in my lap and smooth my skirt. "I grew up in church and surrendered my life early. I married Charles and followed him to seminary. I delivered four little blessings to him, baked bread from scratch, cleaned cloth diapers and counseled women at the local pregnancy support clinic—all while humming hymns."

Imitation mirth ripples around the circle.

"The truth was I masked the loneliness, exhaustion and lost identity of my heart with a smile … because I thought I had to. By the time all four children were fully mobile (and all still under five years old), that mask began to crack. So, I patched it with a vodka veneer."

My past choices constrict my heart, and I yearn to breathe deeply enough to exhale the pain far away.

"For two years I sat in the pew—two children on either side—and beamed up at my husband. Occasional sips from a water bottle kept my smile intact … until the day I ran out. I took a spill in the aisle that set tongues to wagging, opened my husband's eyes and landed me at the altar."

Relief following my admission surprises me. I hear the stories of addiction and guilt around me and allow Pastor Burns' words of comfort and gentle instruction to penetrate my bulwarked being.

Could it be that with the telling—to myself and to others— comes healing?

§

Wildflowers sway beneath the wind's songs. I sit beside the pond and gaze at the splendor nature unfurls around me. The surrounding brightness fades into darkened memories as I recall my final week under alcohol's power.

That Sunday morning, I took more sips than usual to retain my smile. The week had challenged me more than most. Charles' deadline for completion of his doctoral thesis loomed less than a month away. He'd been studying or writing or pastoring for fifteen of his sixteen waking hours, seven days a week. Eight hours were a requirement for sleep—no less. And, of course, he spent about an hour total on eating three square meals.

He liked a big breakfast twenty minutes after he woke at 5:30. Lunch consisted of a protein, two vegetables and a side of pasta. That energized him for the rest of his afternoon's work, study and meetings. Supper could be lighter, but he'd come to expect a fresh-baked dessert. I set that standard during the bliss of our first ten months when the only expectation either of us held for me was to be his wife and homebuilder.

And, honestly, I loved that. I wanted nothing more than to support and encourage him, to create a home of comfort and peace for him to return to after long days of work and study. I found contentment in the life I was building and dismissed advice from wiser women who had been where I was.

"Pray for your husband."

"Fill your own tank in order to fill his."

"Candid communication is key."

I didn't listen. Instead, Charles became the start, finish and middle of my focus, which left little time for me or for God. And then, the children arrived.

As time went on, my husband took a church while continuing his studies. I had our little ones' schedules mapped out to the second so meltdowns would never disturb his evening study time. I ensured they were squeaky clean and dressed appropriately when he got home.

My house remained spotless, and dirty dishes had no place in my sink. I left no unfolded laundry in plain sight or frustration with Charles evident on my face.

I made couponing a science and saved us hundreds of dollars on groceries each month. Charles never knew we couldn't afford to eat the way he wanted. I simply made his expectations reality.

The only times I was away from our children were when I was in the next room at the pregnancy center to lead counseling sessions or when I attended occasional women's weekends if my sister was available to keep the kids.

All my children's needs were met with a smile, a hug and a kiss. I even anticipated needs in the middle of the night, sleeping lightly enough to wake at the softest stirring from them. I would rush to their bedsides before they could disturb the deep-sleeping man beside me.

That Saturday night, our oldest had night terrors off and on for a solid two hours from midnight to 2. The youngest went to the bathroom at 11:20, 1:15 and 3:32.

Charles didn't know any of that happened near him. He'd gone to sleep an hour early at 8:30 so he could wake at 4:30. That schedule allowed him a final sermon review in the pre-Sunday school solitude of the church. After enjoying his sausage, eggs, grits and homemade biscuits, he left a peck on my cheek before slamming the door at 4:50.

He never witnessed the aftereffects of his door closing.

The two youngest—the lightest sleepers—would run into the kitchen, Cheshire grins on their faces, ready for the daily game we played when the door woke them. They hid behind lovies, then popped out—peekaboo! I ducked behind a dish towel—peekaboo! Tiptoe-chase into the bedroom, then snuggle time with mommy—one on either side. Hugs, kisses and back to sleep they'd drift. I'd ease out from between them to get myself ready for church before the older two awoke.

A preacher's wife should look just so. No one noticed, of course, unless I overlooked a stain or smeared my mascara or missed a lump in my unruly hair. I squeezed careful makeovers and dressing into no more than twenty minutes. That's all the time I could find.

No sooner would I have returned to the kitchen than my older children would appear, sleep-tousled and hungry. Once I warmed breakfast, the other two would have joined us. While they gobbled and chatted and giggled, I put our lunch into the crockpot or oven. My family would be starving by the time we got home from church, and none of them wanted to wait for lunch. I made sure they didn't.

Next came dressing four wiggly, opinionated children and overseeing tooth-brushing and hair styling. By the time I had them all strapped into the van, I was exhausted and in desperate need of the water bottle I'd prepared the night before. I considered the clear liquid my reward for somehow getting us to church on time.

On the drive to church, I thought of the tasks still ahead.

Typical Sunday afternoons found me cleaning the kitchen and clipping coupons or making a month's worth of jewelry while everyone else napped. My business, Jewels by Jaida, brought in enough money to make up for any deficit between our food budget and coupons and the rising cost of staples like bacon, steak and sausage. It also allowed me to keep my emergency jugs full.

That Sunday, my exhaustion caught me long before I got close to the work portion.

I drained my bottle before Charles made his third of seven points. Mary and Elizabeth wiggled more than usual. John had dropped his bag of crayons for the third time. On his way to retrieve it, he punched Luke's side. Luke whimpered before I could grasp his arm and give him my warning look. I automatically reached for my bottle and tipped it up. Hands shaking, I lowered it as panic rose. I'd poured the last of my stash that morning since I hadn't been able to get to the liquor store two counties over. Each day that week I'd had extra work typing and editing Charles' dissertation or picking up books he requested from the library.

Panic swelled; my trembling increased. The children grew louder until my inner rumblings overflowed, shattering the patched mask when I screamed at the fidgeting children around me. Shocked at my outburst that interrupted the sermon my husband had worked on for no less than thirty hours that week, I attempted to remove myself and my children from the pew. Instead, I tripped into the aisle facedown, felt my insides churn, pulled myself up by sheer adrenaline and staggered to the nearest restroom where I vomited intermittently for the next fifteen minutes.

I heard all the comments of the sometimes well-meaning, always misguided, gossiping women who peered around the door as I lost all the alcohol I'd consumed and any bit of food I'd managed to sneak in between cleaning, caring and cooking.

"Must be pregnant again."

"Preachers always do have to fill their quivers, don't they?"

"Have you ever seen her rail out like that? To top it off, she tripped over her own two feet, face first!"

"So embarrassing; downright shameful. We have visitors this week!"

In that moment I loathed those women with their false piety and my husband's oblivious self-centeredness. I longed for a drink, a long rest and food and laid my flushed cheek against the cool toilet. Charles found me there after delivering all seven points and the benediction and shaking every churchgoer's hand.

"Jaida? Are you pregnant?"

His question ignited the powder keg of my rage, and all my previously contained anger, frustration and exhaustion exploded.

"No, Charles, damn you! I'm not pregnant; I'm drunk. I've been drunk for two frickin' years. While you've been busy being Jesus' superhero in a robe and hiding in your commentaries and visiting your shut-ins and chatting about doctrine with all your preacher and professor friends and ignoring your family, I've been busy keeping all the daily routines you require running smoothly for you. I've dealt with it all by staying drunk."

With my words mounting an attack upon him, Charles sank beside me in that bathroom stall, and I witnessed his temple for one crumble. The veil he'd hidden himself behind ripped from top to bottom, and I saw a recognition of his own failures in the proof of my own.

He lifted me up in his arms and carried me out of that bathroom, leaving his shortcomings against me and our children to spiral down the toilet with my vomit.

As I recall the way he carried me that day—something he'd never done before—I bring myself back to the present nature. I slide my hand down the stem of the wildflower closest to me and grip near the ground, pulling it up, root and all. I pick flower after flower until I have a full bunch to freshen beneath the waterfall of my face.

They should be enough to replace the dying daisies in the vase on our door.

My shadow's stretched, and I know it must be near supper time. The memory of my life under alcohol's influence kept me longer than I intended. Thank goodness for an extended free time. I realize I needed this emptying of mind and emotion as I pick myself and my flowers up and turn back to our room with its needy vase.

§

"That change you observed in Charles' face—was it an inside metamorphosis? How is he now—toward you, toward your family, toward the needs of all of you?"

I think over the couple of weeks after my disastrous, providential Sunday. Some of that time I spent in the hospital. The church gave Charles an extended vacation, and he obtained an extension on his doctorate. He had to care for the house and kids in my absence. What a disaster I walked into when I got home! He admitted he had no clue how much I did every day. While I was home, he had been more attentive.

"Yes. I do believe it is, but we need a lot of work."

Rose nods and prods me. "What work do you believe he needs?"

"We *both* need it."

Our laughter synchronizes, as she and I reveal we both know her pronoun choice was intentional ... and my response was the one she hoped for.

"I need to open up and talk to him. Be honest; unpack everything I've repressed—intentionally and not—over the years. And, we're going to have to keep communicating when real life starts again."

Pride flashes in Rose's eyes. She recognizes the feeble promise in my answer.

Can I keep it?

"You know this won't be easy. You're realistic, grounded; that's necessary. Do you have someone who can counsel you together when you graduate from here?"

"Pastor Burns will until we find someone in our hometown. Charles has already been talking to him on the phone."

"That's a start. One need we haven't yet discussed is forgiveness." A pang clutches my chest at Rose's mention of the word that haunts my sleepless thoughts. "God has forgiven you. I've held your hand as you've poured out your sins to Him, and you and I both know that God has promised us that, 'If we confess our sins, He is faithful and just to forgive us our sins and to cleanse us from all unrighteousness.'"

I nod. I do know that. As a child, I memorized that verse in I John and have carried it with me throughout my life, repeating it frequently over the past couple months.

"Charles will forgive you. Your children will forgive you. Those are conversations to have, but you and I both know the outcome. They love you; they are supporting you through this. You know that, right?"

This time, the nod releases a drop onto my arm. I know this, too.

"You must forgive Charles, too. I believe you've done this, but you need to say it to him. You've told me about the times you didn't always wake up or you forgot to thaw the chicken or stumbled over a missed toy and ended up with a bruise where you hit the table corner. The fact that Charles never noticed because he didn't see you is something you need to verbalize to him. Any animosity you're clutching must be spoken if you're both moving forward in full honesty. You can't properly forgive what you haven't expressed as something that requires pardon."

I have rehearsed those words in many versions in my head. A grouping of teardrops splashes onto both arms now.

"Jaida, there's a final level to forgiveness. I think you know what it is. I also think you need help to embrace it." Rose cups the top of my hand as she imparts her deeper wisdom.

"Forgive yourself."

My floodgates open now as she continues. "God has forgiven you, wiped you clean. Your sins are removed 'as far as the east is from the west'—gone. Your family will ... likely *has* ... forgiven you. Release that guilt, that shame, that burden. You have no reason to stumble along beneath it. Accept others' forgiveness and forgive yourself."

I sob as I haven't since arriving at the mission. The faces of my family—my husband, each child—flash in my mind. I resented them, dove into a bottle to flee them and my hidden anger toward them. Pigtails, crooked smiles, a chorus of giggles, trusting calls of "Mama!" Each picture in my mind intensifies the sobs racking my body.

"How can I forgive myself for all I've put them through?"

"If the God of the universe—your Creator, Sustainer; the One who saved you from all your sins by giving His own Son's life to bear your punishment—has forgiven you these things, how can you stand against Him in your refusal to forgive yourself?"

My inner breaking shakes my entire body as Rose slides an arm around my convulsing shoulders.

The rush within me subsides. Slows. Ceases. Rose slides a tissue into my palm. I mop up the pieces of the wreckage I'd stubbornly clung to and nod in her direction. Too soon for smiles; I know they'll come, though. One day. The heart pangs have disappeared, in their place, a lightness—freedom.

Rose leans in and whispers, "Healing comes in forgiveness."

§

Shannon sits exactly as I first saw her, draped in another sunbeam. Her hands support the child growing within her. This time, though, a smile illuminates her face as I've never seen it. She greets me when I enter.

"Little Bitty's been kicking up a storm this afternoon."

I sit beside her and slide my hand across her belly. I'm rewarded with a swift kick, and we giggle like no years separate us. Shannon's eyes light up even more as I hand over her favorite chocolate bar. I rip the corner off my own candy bag, and we sink into sugar-laden comfort.

A few moments of silence lead to a sobering of the atmosphere.

"How was your session with Rose today?" Her question reminds me of my breakdown ... and breakthrough.

"Much-needed." I smile before sharing. "I hadn't forgiven myself. As Rose said, forgiveness will usher in more healing; and healing is what I need for myself, for my family—for our future."

Shannon caresses her stomach as she gazes out the window. "We've been talking about the future in my sessions too. I'm thankful to have a future. A few months ago, I didn't. We almost didn't."

She looks down at her child before turning an inquiring gaze to me. I feel her question has been growing for a while. "How? How can I make a good future for this little one? I've made so many mistakes. I feel lost and helpless. Alone."

I catch the first few teardrops as I cup the chin of the terrified young mother before me. "You're never alone. God promises that. Like Pastor Burns told us the other day, we can't sink to a darkness too deep or soar on a high too far for God to reach us."

Shannon's shoulders shake as I hold her in my arms. I flash back to moments in my last few years and feel again the crushing weight of loneliness, the darkness of stumbling along a road I thought I had to walk alone, the hopelessness during the infinite days of no naps, temper tantrums and not enough sleep.

More memories swirl in my mind, and I picture other young mothers around me at the seminary. Covered in spit-up, they wore dark circles beneath eyes that once sparkled. Soft voices rippled across forced smiles with declarations of "So blessed."

Blessed, indeed.

As I remember, I realize how wrong I'd been. They wore masks, too—maybe theirs didn't require alcohol to remain intact, but masks nonetheless. Also, I was never alone. Not only did God never abandon me, the other moms around me likely had many of the same fears, frustrations and faith-draining days I did—struggles common to us all, to Shannon.

"You will never be alone with God. You also never have to be alone in your mother journey." I serve the kernels of truth popping within me. "Being a mother is exhausting. It will never be easy, but it is a call—a mighty one. You don't have to have it all together; you don't even need to have most of it together. Many days, you'll be positive you don't have any of it together. Regardless, you will not be alone because moms like me ... like your mom ... have been there. Whatever each new day brings—good, bad, in between—call us, and we'll be there with chocolate or hugs or tissues ... and prayers, always."

I hold her as fears release from her heart. I silently pray for her salvation, upcoming delivery, future, child, parents. As her pain subsides and she sits back, I take her hands in mine and speak, mother to mother.

"Other mothers have been there. We love you and want to rejoice with you, grieve with you, rage with you—whatever you need." Hope spreads in Shannon's eyes. "Even if we can't physically be there, God will never leave you."

She squeezes my hands. "Will you pray with me before we head to supper? I want to get there early and see if I can snag two bowls of pudding."

We laugh. I pray. She smiles.

"Thank you. I do believe what you said about God. I've been working through that, too, in sessions with Rose. I've been listening to Pastor Burns in group and chapel. I'm kind of looking forward to worship tonight."

My heart warms as I pray again that my roommate will accept Christ as her Savior and follow God into her new future. As we walk to the cafeteria, I think how precious it would be to call her my sister in Christ.

I reflect on our conversation and my memories. With all I've been through and all I've put myself and my family through, I want to be there for other women like me. What a privilege it would be to help others cast away their masks and not live out the mistakes I made.

What could the church look like if we all showed our faces—no makeup, no covered scars? What could that look like for our children? Mothers hold the future of the church in a unique way, so what if we show that future the truth of our pasts in our present?

No filters. Not alone—together. With God.

§

I've looked forward to this day and feared it.

Some invisible force grips my feet as I inch toward the picnic table nearest the pond. His back is to me, and I feel butterflies—like when we first met and started dating. Our wedding day and night, the butterflies fluttered.

It's been a lifetime since then. My hands feel damp, shaky; I run them along my pant legs. I'm hopeful and hopeless all at once. Ducks fly in and glide onto the water's surface.

Charles shifts to watch them. In his profile, I see love. I see life. I see future.

Our love. Our life. Our future.

Other feelings bubble within me, complicated yet simple. Love, passion, forgiveness, regret, joy, sorrow, desire, hope.

Charles notices me and turns while rising. In his eyes, I catch a reflection of all my emotions. He and his lips meet me and mine. In the eternity of our kiss, our hearts and souls converse. I frame his face and taste his love. Somewhere along with my voice, my passion for him and us died. But today ...

Today's our resurrection day.

We emerge for air, and he parts the silence with a whisper of my name. Just my name, but he encompasses so much promise in it. He sees me. Uttering his name in return opens the floodgates of my words, and all my heart's desires rush out.

"I need you to see me every day, but I need to see you too. Both of us need to paint the other a picture when we're unable to see ourselves—the good and the bad. I need help stripping away the wallpaper I've plastered around us. It's time to bare the walls of our relationship and restore them ... together."

His eyes radiate honesty and sorrow in his admission.

"I hate myself for not seeing you. For not recognizing all you did for me—all I made you think you had to do—and for the incredible burden you carried alone. I'm supposed to be a shepherd, yet I failed in that role with the most important people God's put in my life. Please forgive me."

His hands on my cheek and in the depths of my hair remind me of the way he used to touch me, see me, feel me—and the way I used to touch, see and feel him.

He continues. "I see you now, and I never want to stop. You're no longer alone. I'll be the partner you should have always had by your side. I'll rebuild and move forward with you. Our future will be so much better than our past because we won't forsake our Cornerstone—Christ. I promise you that. My beautiful Jaida."

Cheeks together, our tears mingle as promises and love flow. I long to splash in the brook of our passions. He stirs me— body, heart and soul—and I vow to do the same for him.

§

"I want other women, especially young mothers, to know they're not alone. That might be one of the top lie darts Satan pierces us with."

No tears during my session with Rose today.

"You're glowing today, Jaida; and I praise God for these future-thinking words tumbling out of your mouth! You are so right. Loneliness is one of the top issues I hear from women."

Rose's smile and positivity spread over me, and I share my heart.

"I know not every day will be easy, and I'm not entirely sure how to nurture this plan blossoming in my heart. But, I am basking in the confidence that God's gifted me and resting in the promise that He knows His plan for me. He's brought me out of my figurative seventy years in Babylon, and I want to be His light as I return to my world."

"I believe you will. He's placed this desire in your heart. When God does that, He also guides to make it a reality."

Her joy matches mine, and I'm eager to run headlong into this hope-filled future.

§

Peace rests on my shoulders like the fleece blankets I scatter around our house. Its warming comfort fills me, and I reflect on the past few months as I glance around our circle again. Shannon, Pete, Jack. Each of us has made strides in our recovery journeys. God is greater than any drug, pill or bottle. I know that. I thank God I've seen that acceptance and belief in at least two of the others. The thought of the night Shannon accepted Christ still fills my heart with joy.

Jack's laughter at Pastor Burns' joke reaches his eyes today. I smile as he looks my way, shaking his unruly bangs from the eyes he no longer keeps pinned to his shoes. Though he doesn't know, my smile is a prayer—for him, for his future, for his salvation. Pete's chuckle and soft gaze at his young roommate show me our prayers for Jack are united.

I cling to the understanding I've gained over the past few weeks. My prayer repeats a plea for God to guide me in using my recovery for Him when I return home, where real life resumes as I face all those who never knew my pain and who might be hiding their own.

The fullness of my heart spills over my lashes as I think of the opportunities before all of us. I give thanks for the freedom I find in understanding that the Christian life doesn't mean perfection. It's daily sin and forgiveness—stumbling over myself but being picked up by my heavenly Father.

Pastor Burns opens our final group session with prayer, and I bow my head. He charges and encourages us and presents us the opportunity to share our plans for outside this haven.

"I'm ready to go home and get some hugs and kisses from my babies." I smile at the mental image of all four children running into my arms when I emerge from the car at home. "God's got a plan for everything—even the sinful choices we make. I will use my story to help other women who feel lost and alone and tired and fed up but don't think they can admit their truth and reality. I want them to see that's normal. It's human. We're human, but God ... well, he's God! He'll carry us through when we turn all our cares over to Him. I'm done with the mask; I'm ready to be open and honest—relatable and accessible—for those who need an example of joy on the other side of forgiveness."

Look of Promise

My finger circles the smooth curve of the shutter button as I adjust focus on the groom's face. My ears lock in on the church doors behind me. I swear I hear the swoosh of air as the bride's nephews open them, followed by the collective intake of breaths across the cathedral's expanse. And then, my work begins.

His first glimpse. Shock, emotions overflow.

Love. *Click.*

Zoom in. Reaction. *Click.*

Closer. The tear, unchecked. *Click.*

The smile, true. *Click.*

The look. *Click, click.*

The Look.

My emotions stick in my throat. *Not today.* I swallow, silently clear my throat. Focus.

Best man passes a handkerchief. *Click.* Laughter. *Click.* Teasing. *Click.*

Bride enters the frame. The look that passes. *Click.*

Father gives her away. *Click.* More tears. Hands pass. *Click.*

"Dearly beloved ..."

§

I remember the first time a guy looked at me—noticed, showed interest. I basked in that look. He was a few years older, and I stood on top of the world because he'd picked me. So, when he whispered in my ear and took my hand, I followed.

When he pushed me down, I complied. When his hands took over, I let them. When it hurt, I swallowed the pain and whispered what I thought he wanted to hear. When it was over, I didn't question where the look had gone.

I was thirteen.

That began my first addiction—a constant need for the high a look brought. I ignored the pains of withdrawal and found ways to keep the looks coming. Drugs soon followed.

A few months later, a look from a stranger brought a sweeping promise: more drugs—a never-ending supply—and appreciation. I jumped in the pickup truck and didn't look back.

My parents didn't get to celebrate my fourteenth birthday.

§

"Do you?"

"I do." *Click.*

"Do you?"

"I do." *Click.*

Teardrop falls. *Click, click.*

Three mouthed words. Two smiles. One future.

Click, click, click.

§

"I don't want …"

The sound of his slap punched my eardrum before the sting of his hand burned my cheek. I opened my eyes to the new look—the one that commanded, demanded, dominated.

I submitted to the needles so I could say, "I do." To the clients. To the drugs. To the life.

Was that life?

§

"I promise you my life, myself, my all." *Click.*

"For better, for worse …." *Click, click.*

"In sickness, in health …." *Click, click.*

"For as long as we both shall live." *Click.*

§

"How'd it go?"

I toss my camera bags on the hotel bed and smile at Rachael. Once upon a time, I would have rolled my eyes at the idea of being best friends with a preacher's daughter.

"I got all the great shots: the cake, the kiss, the vows. The Look."

Rachael drapes her arm across my shoulders as I sink next to her. We've discussed my love-hate relationship with capturing grooms' first looks at their brides. The thing is, despite all my experience with looks, I've never been on the receiving end of the kind I capture with my camera's lens.

I don't expect to ever be.

Rachael rests her head on mine, and we sit in silence for a few minutes.

"Can I tell you something?"

"You can tell me."

I dish out my response with a side of laughter at our often-repeated dialogue.

"Will you listen?"

"I make no promises!"

Our smiles recede as we face one another, and I watch seriousness replace Rachael's teasing.

"One day, you will receive a look unlike any you've seen before. It will be meant for you alone. And ..."

I attempt to will away my emotion as I sense the direction of her words. The doubts and fears and truths I've wrestled over the years force their way out of my depths as Rachael enfolds my hands in hers.

"Please hear me out, Shannon."

I make myself look back at the girl who became my friend before I was fit to be one back. She broke through my hatred and anger and made me accept the help my parents eagerly offered.

My parents never stopped searching, praying. The entire time I was enslaved, they followed leads, posted photos and urged law enforcement agencies across the country to search for their daughter. I'd like to say I thanked them when I was rescued; instead, I fought them. I fought recovery. I fought my future.

Rachael fought for me.

She was there when they brought me home from the hospital the first time. Officers had found me in a condemned apartment building in Memphis, passed out with two other girls on a paper-thin mattress stained with decades of atrocities. A needle dangled from my arm.

They rushed me to the emergency room and nearly killed me before slowly raising my body—and my unborn daughter—from the grave.

It was my soul the doctors had no machines to salvage.

My first steps staggered me straight to the drugs I thought I had to have and landed me in custody. My parents continued to pray and plead and take me to counseling, but I wanted none of it and ran away a few times.

The last time, I didn't run far, simply entered the woods behind my parents' house with a broken mirror and a jagged desire to end my pain. Another hospital visit brought Rachael to my side where she stayed until I listened.

Like then, I focus on my friend's words.

"You may shake your head at me and try to ignore what I'm about to say, but, Shannon, deep down you know I'm speaking truth. You gave your life to God in that mission chapel five years ago. Christ's blood covers all your sins and past. God looks at you as you are—His child. He soothes the scars, wipes your tears and ... He sees *you*.

"One day you will be seen with human eyes full of love and truth, too. Right now, though, you need to learn to give the look you desire to yourself. When you look in the mirror, do you see the new you—the girl who was saved from a living death to the promise of eternal life? That's who you should see."

I hate crying in front of anyone. Weakness could have meant a death sentence where I was imprisoned for more than two years, so I learned to suppress emotions.

With Rachael, though, tears are safe. She exemplifies true friendship and teaches me that weakness is made perfect through God's strength.

My friend remained beside me through rehab and the mission, my daughter's delivery and our weaning from the drugs I'd hooked us both on before Laylah was born. Rachael stood nearby while my parents and I healed and as I proved myself worthy of being a mother to the little girl who survived it all. She saw my photography dream and helped me realize it.

And, right now, she's sobbing with me, as she lays out truths I need to hear but can't tell myself.

"One day, when the time is right, you will gaze into that look you long for; and it will be right and beautiful and pure and everything you've never allowed yourself to dream. That will happen because, before then, you will understand the way God sees you and you will have learned to see yourself that way too. Your past will not matter to that special man because he will love *you*. The you he sees. The you whose past he will love away, whose scars he will kiss and whose future he will embrace."

All the tissues are gone. I throw the empty box at her, and we laugh the lingering sadness away.

I look again at my friend.

"Thank you."

§

Seasons of growth in Christ's love and confidence in His plan for me come and go.

Rachael travels with me to Augusta for another wedding. All the men in the wedding party play golf, so we take portraits on a golf course. Rachael keeps Laylah busy on the nearby playground. I promised them ice cream between here and the nighttime wedding.

As usual, I cover the groom's side while my partner, Trevor, handles the bride's. We shoot our way through the desired portraits from full party, down to the happy couple and their closest friends. The maid of honor is the bride's sister. Trevor has them cheesing it up on the putting green, while I direct the groom and best man to a tee box.

"Okay, Jackson, do you and your buddy ..."

"Matthew."

I smile. "Do you and Matthew have any inside jokes or goofy shots you'd like to recreate here, once we get some frame-worthy ones for your bride?"

"How about I rest my head on a tee while he sets up to drive it to the green?"

I laugh. Guys in weddings often reveal warped senses of humor, not to mention overabundant immaturity.

"Let's do one with the handshake after your talented photographer here makes us look respectable."

I look at the best man for the first time.

Sure, as a photographer, I size up every member of the wedding party and frame them appropriately in each shot. I know who blinks at the worst times, who requires a candid snap for genuine smiles and who's going to cause extra edits. I rarely look any closer—beyond the lens, so to speak—at the people I photograph.

Especially the groomsmen.

I learned early in my career that closer examination resulted in flashbacks or panic attacks as I envisioned them in the blurry myriad of faces sneering down on me during my captivity.

This time, though, something in Matthew's voice calls me to see him. A warmth blooms in my heart, which misses a beat, and I look away.

Did I just blush?

I survive their portraits and pray neither of them noticed my shaky hands as I internally remind myself I am a professional. I assist Trevor with the reflectors and the bride with her hair and dress as he photographs the couple.

We frame the final couple portraits in a golf cart near the club house. I hear Laylah's shouts of "Mama!" and wave. As soon as we're done, I nod to Rachael, and they skip my way.

Laylah leaps into my arms and chatters nonstop about the lion and giraffe she rocked on at the playground and how she swung higher than Auntie Rach. I make fun of my friend and laugh at her faked offense. That's when I notice we've gained an audience.

Matthew hands me the lens cap I didn't realize I had dropped.

"You might need this later this evening." His smile causes another heart malfunction, and I realize I forgot to breathe. "Thanks for being so patient with all of us, especially my goofball friend."

"It was nothing."

I have no idea why I say that or if that's really what I say or if I say anything out loud.

"Do you like lions or giraffes better?" Laylah's got her hands on her hips, her face stern, as she poses her question to this stranger.

Matthew kneels before her and matches her expression. "That's a tough question. I think I'd have to say ... lions."

"Why?" One hand drops from her hip, while the other forms a fist.

"Because I like to hear them roar."

"That's a good answer." Satisfied, my daughter flashes one of her famous sunny smiles and high-fives him with her now unclenched hand.

Matthew stands and issues another smile my way. "Your daughter asked a great question."

My laugh sounds awkward to my ears. "She does that."

"She does that?" What kind of response is that? And now I'm blushing ... again.

I search the ground for a magical sinkhole and wonder when the mild autumn weather turned mid-summer sauna-ish.

Matthew's smile broadens, and he waves as he jogs to rejoin the happy couple. "See you tonight!"

"Tonight?"

I repeat the word as a question because I forget that I am a photographer with a wedding to shoot that evening. *Maybe he didn't hear me.* The second I turn toward Rachael, she bursts out laughing—hands-on-knees, bent double, rolling laughter—at me.

"Come on, Laylah. Time for ice cream." I storm off, my cheeks on fire and my heart beating out of my chest. "Aunt Rach doesn't get any."

§

I'm in my usual spot near the front of the church. The groom stands centered in my viewfinder.

All the groomsmen have advanced to their spots. I zoom out to capture them all. *Click, click, click.*

I zoom back in, readjust my focus. Nearly time. I angle my neck like I always do to listen for the opening of the doors. Zoom a little more. My breath catches, and I ease the camera away from my face.

Matthew's looking directly at me.

I gaze over the camera before me, straight back at him. I smile and, again, I blush. I duck behind my camera.

Zoom in. Focus on the reaction. *Click.*

Closer. The smile, genuine. *Click.*

The Look.

Click, click.

Never before have I missed a groom's first look, but … the one I captured?

Its promise was meant for me.

Life of Purpose

I've always wondered how the end will be. Never imagined it would sit a spell with me and my recollections.

As I lie here alone in the bed my wife and I have shared most of our days, I think back. About my family, friends, addiction and wake-up call.

Most of all, I consider my purpose.

I shift to cough. I never knew something so simple could feel like a knife slicin' my lungs. Despite my surety I won't find another breath, my reflexes suck one in.

As the pain oh-so-slowly subsides, I focus on my last thought—purpose.

My one regret is how little time I gave it. My stubbornness blinded me from truth until late in my days.

Once I saw, though—boy howdy, did I feel like a young buck! Even my Cynthia giggled at how spry and full of oats I was after my time in the mission. It was about mid-way through there when I knew all I wanted to do was tell others bout Jesus and what He'd done for me.

The first time I saw someone come to the Lord was in prison. I had a sentence to pay for my mistakes, though the judge reduced it more than I deserved.

Course, it was the Judge of the universe who'd given me far more grace than I deserved. Pastor Ben always quoted his wife to us: "None of us deserves any good thing." Wish I could've met that wise little lady. She and my Cynthia would've got along right well, I reckon.

Cynthia ... where is she?

Clinks and gentle hummin' tell me she's fixin' my breakfast. Saint of a woman, that one. She prayed for me every day. Never stopped and said, "Thank you, Jesus! I knew it would be any time now," when I told her I'd turned my life on over to her God.

Course, then she corrected me with "*our* God."

My chuckle nearly sends me into another fit of coughin', and I close my eyes to seek out any breaths still comin' my way. They drift in, slowly ... one by half of one.

Back to my memory of seein' someone come to Christ: Ricky was his name, another kid. It's funny as I recollect—two roommates in a row were young'uns. They bunked me with Jack Calhoun at the mission. He's one I still pray for ev'ry day.

Ricky, he got busted for stealin'. Problem was, he wasn't just takin'. He pointed a gun at a man. He'd been in and out of juvie for years already. All that combined to make him do adult time. Slowly, Ricky started talkin' to me. Turns out, he was stealin' for his kid brothers. Their mama was on the meth.

He couldn't find a steady job to hire him. He'd been tryin' to keep him and his brothers in school and out of the system so they could stay together. Problem was—enough food and shoes without holes didn't come cheap for growin' boys.

In the rack above me, the kid cried himself to sleep ev'ry night, worried sick over his brothers. They'd been split up; he didn't know where.

He got low. Asked me one day, "What's the point, man? Why bother with this jacked up life?"

I held up my Bible. Told him, "This."

He listened to me, let me share what I was readin' ev'ry day. 'Fore long I was sharin' thoughts on what we were readin', answerin' questions he had. We were goin' through the book of John and got to Jesus' death. He kept me up most of that night with questions needin' answers until that young man, tears rollin', knelt on the floor of that jail cell and prayed for Jesus to take over his life.

That was his seventeenth birthday.

I spoke with a lawyer and social worker and preacher. We got his sentence shortened, found his brothers and found one home willin' to take all five of 'em. Ricky led his brothers to Jesus, too.

He calls a few times a week.

I glance at the phone. It'll ring in a couple hours. Ricky's found a graveyard shift that pays pretty well to go along with another nighttime cleanin' job. He likes to call once he's had some food and is ready for a few hours of sleep. He'll need it to help him stay awake during homework time with his youngest brothers.

By the phone, my Bible's still open from last night's readin'. Takes me some doin' to work my arm over there and heave it back. My other arm turns it around easier, but I forgot my readin' glasses on the nightstand.

Never mind. I know where I've been readin'—Psalm 52. I don't need to see the words on the thumb-worn pages; they appear in my mind.

"I am like a green olive tree in the house of God; I trust in the mercy of God forever and ever. I will praise you forever because you have done it; and in the presence of your saints I will wait on your name, for it is good."

It is good, indeed.

Since servin' my time, I've traveled across the southern United States, spreadin' God's word. Whenever I speak, folks pour down the aisle after ... or shuffle along the gray concrete of the prison. Some rededicate their lives; some give their lives to Christ for the first time; others hug my neck. Lots of 'em stay late into the night, sharin', cryin', prayin'.

In the prisons, some wardens notice the dif'rence when I speak and let me stick around. I don't mind bein' behind bars now. God's message brings freedom beyond time and space.

Prisons, churches, buses—God works ev'rywhere. A few years back, I was ridin' the Greyhound clear out to Texas. Lord knows I was tired. I thought I needed sleep; God had other ideas. This fella beside me starts pourin' out his sins ... reckon maybe he thought I was a priest when I told him I was headin' to speak at a church.

'Fore I could adjust my neck pillow and close my eyes on him, he's confessin' it all—adultery, insider tradin', hidden accounts. I wondered what I'd do if he started givin' me burial spots.

Next thing I know, the guy's weepin' like a baby. I hand him my handkerchief and place a hand on his shoulder. I'm prayin' silently over him, askin' God for words to give this fella. The man calms down, wipes his face and stares right out the window at the pastureland flashin' past us. I barely hear his whispered words, but I thank God I did.

"It'll all be over soon."

My breathin's comin' slower now ... maybe 'cause of my current memory—thinkin' how close he was to his end.

After that man's whispered resignation, God opened my mouth. He used my clumsy ol' words to let the man beside me know the God who created him's got a plan for him. I shared Pastor Ben's words, "You can never do more bad than God can forgive."

I told him God's bigger than his worst sins, and it's never too late to start new. Like me.

By the time we rolled into Galveston, that man—Bobby's his name—had got down on his knees, between seats in that smelly ol' bus, and confessed it all again to the only One's got the power to forgive. He told me he'd planned to return to his family's land and kill himself. Instead, he was walkin' straight off that bus to a phone to beg his wife's forgiveness and then to the nearest police station to turn himself in.

He still calls once or twice a year. His wife and kids forgave him, stood by him; and now they've got a new life together.

Thinkin' of beautiful lives brings to mind my family. Their images keep me from needin' to breathe for a bit. As I flip through the photos in my mental wallet, I remember ev'ry few pictures to pull in just one more breath.

A beautiful face. Another. Another. One more breath.

More faces I know better'n my own. Slower, but one more breath follows.

Next, the faces of those who've come to Christ—my family in Him.

God let me walk alongside so many of His children as they got to know Him. I didn't mind those tears—happy, thankful, rejoicin' ones.

Beats grievin' tears—grievin' over causin' others pain.

God knows I've cried those, too.

Durin' the last several months of driving the semi, I rode a carousel of pills. I needed 'em to either stay awake for runs longer than my logs showed or for sleep on demand. I'd fought double vision and leg numbness for months. There'd been a few close calls, but I couldn't—wouldn't—hang up the CB.

Before a late-night run crossin' Arizona, the pills had kept me asleep longer than they should, so I took some extras to keep me up and runnin'. I'd have to drive straight through and push the speed to make my deadline.

I'd just come out of slowin' down through a speed trap. I shot thanks up to the God I didn't believe in that truckers still looked out for each other. We'd alert the brothers in our wake to radar guns.

Once I accelerated to my preferred speed, I glanced down at the family picture I kept taped to my dash. My truck had put four kids through college. My youngest, Sarah Lynn, had just had her third baby: little stairsteps they were—4, 2 and 3 months. I was chucklin' at the thought of my girl pregnant. She'd always been a bit of a beanpole; pregnant, she was a beanpole with a bean pod pokin' out.

That's when I saw the taillights.

My foot had clamped down; I hadn't even realized. I was goin' too fast. And my leg was numb.

It took both my hands to move my right leg off the accelerator. My left leg sprang to action, clampin' down on the brake as I worked the wheel and shifter. The semi jackknifed; the trailer started to tip. The minivan's driver veered left—too late.

With the impact, the van spun like a top before comin' to rest against the guardrail on the right side.

My breathin's not wantin' to come through this memory. My vision's startin' to fade black around the edges, then I find a stray bit of air and keep rememberin'.

No one had been seriously injured. Anyone who saw that wreck had to come away believin' in miracles. I reckon that family's guardian angels had lined up to take the brunt of the impact—one for each person: dad, mom, and three kids ... ages 4, 2 and 3 months.

Even without a court order, I'd never have slid behind the wheel again. Retirement caught me that night, and I hit my knees.

My prayers had been full of thanks for God sparin' the lives of that family. Every time I look at my Sarah Lynn and her babies, I see that family, and I thank God again.

The breathin' aches worse now, even though it's not really comin' ... not all the way deep anyway. It's shallow. I don't have much longer.

Instead of the panic I always expected, I feel warm and safe, like being tucked in tight beneath my great-grandmother's hand-stitched quilt. Those images fill my mind again ... all at once now. I'm picturin' my wife, my four kids and their spouses, all ten of my grandbabies, my family in God.

A whisper spreads through my mind. It's a voice I've never heard audibly yet know better than my own. As it continues, I think maybe I have heard it my entire life.

"I will watch over them. Junior will keep sharing your story across the nation. Cindy and Jackson and their families will stay close by Cynthia and look out for her until she falls asleep in my arms. Sarah Lynn's got one more baby on the way; she and Bryant will find out tonight. All your grandbabies will serve me, too. They are my lambs, and I will keep them in my fold all their days."

I know now what the end is.

It's not an end. It's a beginnin'. Bright, beautiful. Peace and joy like I've never known.

"My Savior and my King."

I bow.

"Well done, good and faithful servant. Enter into the joy of your Lord."

Legacy of Tenacity

"If any of you lacks wisdom, let him ask of God, who gives to all liberally and without reproach, and it will be given to him. But let him ask in faith, with no doubting, for he who doubts is like a wave of the sea driven and tossed by the wind."
James 1:5-6

Pride, Burned

Public speaking has never been my thing. All I remember from high school speech class is paralyzing terror. I glance at the audience. Way more folks stare at me now than back in that classroom a lifetime ago.

Surely they hear my heart pounding as loudly as I do. The backs of my knees suddenly become damp, and I doubt they'll support my weight when my introduction is over and I'm expected to stand and walk to the podium—or pulpit, I suppose it's called in a church.

"Join me in welcoming my new friend, Jed!"

Ducky's broad smile and energetic clapping calm my nerves, but I still feel shaky as we share a shoulder bump on my way to the microphone. I scan the sea of smiles before me but see beyond those masks. Their eyes reveal sympathy and, often, discomfort.

I clear my throat and remember the terror on my children's faces when they first saw me after the accident. The gnarly scars covering my face and neck are bad enough. Add in the empty sleeves that my sweet Lana pins to my shoulders, and you've got a living, walking, talking freak show. I glance down for a moment and ask the God I'm starting to understand for a shot of courage to share our story.

"Ducky asked me to share how my family and me got here and what we've been through. So, I figure the best place to start would be toward my beginning.

"Growing up, it was drilled into me that the man provides for his family. He cares for them and protects them. My daddy did it. His daddy before him did it. I aimed to do it as well ... and I did for a while. Lana, there ..."

I nod to the front pew where my wife sits beside her friend Daisy.

"She and I had been sweet on each other since fifth grade. Our senior year, we were the couple you hear about in country songs. I was quarterback; she was a cheerleader. We got voted homecoming king and queen.

"As the refs blew their whistles for halftime of our homecoming game, I ran to the field house to wipe off some sweat and switch to my suit. When I got back, there she was—in the pinkest, poofiest dress I'd ever seen—sitting on the homecoming court platform over the fifty-yard line. Her smile was bigger than usual, but I knew it was about to get even bigger ... at least, I hoped it would.

"I nodded to Mr. Duncan, the band director, to start playing mine and Lana's favorite song. The band marched behind me and fanned out while I climbed the steps to cross the platform and kneel in front of her. With the band rocking out behind us and our whole town cheering from the stands, I asked her to be my wife and make me the luckiest fellow alive. That smile did grow, and she said yes."

Lana's blushing, but I see her love for me as clear as I did way back then. Her nod encourages me.

"She jumped in my arms. While I spun her around, I whispered that I would always love, protect and care for her; that she'd never want for anything in my arms—an ironic promise, as you can see."

Nervous laughter spreads through the crowd. I'm an acquired taste to look at these days; self-deprecating humor sometimes speeds the process.

"The day after graduation was our wedding, and we ran headlong into the adult world. We got ourselves set up fairly well a few hours from our hometown. We rented a small house from some distant kinfolk. A few years later, we decided to expand our family. The second line on that little stick had us dancing around our living room. When the doctor gave us the news that we'd be getting two for the price of one, though, I had to take a seat to let it sink in.

"Double the clothes and diapers and baby gear. I was determined they'd have the best of everything, though. For a few months while Lana was pregnant, I took on a second job to save for the extra expenses coming. Just after Travis and Jenna were born, I got a new construction job that paid better than I'd been making. Finally, life was rolling like I'd always planned. I had my family, a decent job. It was time for me to set us up better with our own land and a car that'd been made in this century. We took on a mortgage and a car note, but I had a plan and made sure we didn't borrow more than my salary could cover.

"When the babies were a couple years old, we hit a season of loss. Lana and I only had four living parents and grandparents between us when we got married, and we lost all of them in the space of ten months.

"That hit me hard. Without the presence of my daddy and granddaddy, I could no longer pick up the phone for needed advice or reminders of how a man should be. I felt like I'd been dropped in the wilderness at night without a compass, map or flashlight.

"Neither of us had siblings, and what family we had left weren't close and were unable to be a net for us in the event of a catastrophe. We didn't have a community like y'all here at Sovereign Grace. I didn't think we needed one. Lana and I were totally on our own for the first time in our lives. Little did I know what was coming a few years later."

I bow my head and swallow a few times. It occurs to me how awkward it would be to cry on stage without hands to wipe tears away. I take a few deep breaths and pray again for God's help.

"For a long time, I didn't remember much about that afternoon. Most of it has come back in bits and pieces. Where we lived, our neighbors weren't overly well off. They got by, and that's about it. One of them would come around every so often to 'borrow' some gasoline for his mower. I didn't mind and was happy I could help others now and then.

"That afternoon, he came over with his glass jar so he could mow his lawn. I was busy pushing the twins on their swing set we'd got them earlier that year for their fourth birthday. I hollered, 'You know where it's at,' and didn't think much more about it. After supper, I went out to my shop to cut some metal tubes for the industrial shelving I was making for our garage. I set up my grinder, put on my safety goggles and got to work.

"What I didn't know was my neighbor'd put his jar up on my worktable to pour in the gas. He'd spilled a bunch and grabbed my shop rags to soak up the mess. I didn't notice them sitting there, though, before I went to letting sparks fly. It didn't take many to send the pile up in flames. I tried to knock the flaming mess down onto the concrete, but the fire leapt up my arms instead.

"Now, I should have noticed the rags that didn't belong. I should have smelled the gasoline. So many 'should haves,' but I didn't. It was late; I was tired and determined to finish those cuts because I had to be on a job site early the next morning. To make matters worse, when it happened, I stepped backward into a big shelf loaded down with wood and paint cans and other heavy materials. When I bumped into it, something fell and knocked me to the ground, unconscious, while the fire burned me alive."

Looks of shock and gasps of horror reach me, and I feel a shift in the emotions of the crowd as I take the first turn in my story.

"Thank goodness Lana came out right then with a glass of her sweet, cold lemonade. Without her quick reaction, none of us would be here today. I can't remember much of anything except pain until a couple months later when I realized I was in a hospital and they'd taken both my arms. The burns on them were too deep for anything to be saved. They did grafts on my chest and neck. My face had the least amount of damage—as you can see by these righteous scars."

Tilting my head side to side to model the marks, I notice the audience's reaction isn't as uncertain as my previous joke. It seems humor does help people come to grips with my appearance. When I speak again, I nod toward my wife.

"Lana's the one with deeper scars. She found me in the flames. I know she still dreams about that day; her nightmares kill me."

I fight against tears again and push on with our story.

"There she was: two young kids to care for; a husband who she wasn't sure would even live, ringing up a massive medical bill every day while his job and insurance vanished. Without my income, she started taking all the odd jobs she could while still caring for the kids. They transported me to a hospital about an hour away, so she couldn't see me every day. When she visited, I saw the burden of it all resting heavy on her shoulders. She cried when she told me she wanted nothing more than to be with me every day, but she'd only be able to get there once a week or so.

"With the little bit she was able to make, Lana kept the kids fed and paid toward my medical bills. As my stay in the hospital stretched on, the car was the first to go. Lana apologized to me through tears when she told me she couldn't pay the note and feed the kids. Her choice meant she'd rarely see me anymore. All I wanted to do was hold her hand and wrap my arms around her, but I couldn't even do that. I felt completely helpless ... and hopeless.

"Nearly a year after my accident, the twins started kindergarten, so Lana was able to get a steadier job with longer hours. By then, the damage was done. When you live in a small town you didn't grow up in and the bank president who holds your mortgage has a son with his eye on your property, you don't stand much of a chance of receiving grace once you get more than a few months behind in your payments. Lana took a couple days off work to find a rental place she could afford and to get everything moved before they were evicted.

"I had no idea how bad things were for my family. I was giving all I could to rehab, trying desperately to learn how to live without arms. At the time, I was also seesawing between wanting to learn how to function and longing to eat a bullet. It was probably best I didn't know how bad things had gotten. I probably would've chosen the bullet. With me gone, Lana could move on and not be tied down by the half-man I'd become.

"People say I'm lucky to be alive, lucky the doctors kept me from dying. They brought me back from the dead alright. Back to our checking and meager savings depleted, our house and car taken and no way to afford more therapy or any kind of fancy prosthetics. Back to a world where wanted ads don't ask for armless guys."

The sour of bitterness rises in my throat as those early emotions return. I see Lana wipe away tears and give thanks for the friend holding her hand.

"Sometimes I wonder how it might've been different had we not lost our family. They would have cared for Lana and the kids. We might not have lost everything. They would have advised us on how to avoid losing all our insurance and helped us fight the bank. Of course, I'm not sure anything—even the wisdom of my dad and granddad—could have prepared me for how to provide for and protect my family with a burned body and no arms.

"Just before the hospital released me, Lana got the final blow. While she was at work and the kids were at school, an electrical fire broke out and took down their entire duplex and part of the one next to it. We still think the owner was looking for an easy out from his own mortgage on the properties, but we couldn't prove that. All Lana knew at the time was she had no home to return to with our babies. Again, she missed work to hunt for another place. No one would rent to her without two or three months paid up front. She had just spent all the pennies she'd saved on an old junk car, so she'd have something to bring me home in. The only problem was, we no longer had a home.

"The firemen salvaged one thing from the fire—our safe with important papers. Everything else was destroyed. Lana shopped at the thrift store for as many necessities as she could—blankets and pillows and a few kitchen supplies. She focused grocery shopping on the canned food aisle. She and the kids 'camped' in the car and dined on canned meats and cold beans. Two days later, she picked me up from the rehab. The old car couldn't go much over 40, so we had a while together before we finally got back to town to pick our kids up from school. Christmas break began the following day, and we had a lot of decisions to make.

"Without a home, we assumed the state would take our children from us. We decided to find somewhere safe and out of sight of prying eyes to keep the car—our new home on wheels—until we could get back on our feet. When we picked the kids up, though, their teacher was waiting with them. The kids had told her about living in the car, and she was there to inspect our loaded down junker and express her concerns. Lana turned on her homecoming queen smile and told the teacher we had been playing make believe with the kids. In reality, she said, we were taking a long road trip for the holidays to visit friends in another state.

"The teacher didn't look entirely convinced. We worried she would call the authorities and panicked. We didn't consider there might be programs that would help our family or that the state wouldn't take the kids because we didn't have an address. All we knew was we had just reunited after fourteen months and had no intention of being separated again.

"Lana and I decided to find somewhere farther away until we could figure out what to do long-term. We went toward Durham, North Carolina, figuring a bigger city would allow us to blend in. That began our first winter living in a car. We weren't prepared for how cold it would be."

I take a breath as I think through all the things I could have done differently—of how honesty might have saved us the heartbreak to come without jeopardizing our family's togetherness.

"Over the holidays, we moved the car around during the day, parking near playgrounds for a few hours at a time. The kids enjoyed that. They missed their swing set. We knew things could get more complicated once school started again.

"Lana took the car to look for work. Without an address, it was difficult to apply for typical jobs. She scraped together a little of the last money we had and made some business cards. She could clean people's houses and small businesses in areas that would be easy to reach through public transportation.

"Talk about a punch to my gut: watching my wife's soft hands become rough and chapped from cleaning fancy homes so we could have food and gas—because I no longer had hands. Whenever her fingers frame my messed-up face, I kiss those beautiful, selfless hands. Many folks would've told her to leave me long ago, but she was determined to keep us going— together."

Daisy slides her arm around Lana's shoulders, and I smile at them. I will never stop thanking my wife for her sacrifices through all we've survived.

"Feeling useless and helpless became the daily norm for me, but even that would get worse. We found ourselves in a few situations where I worried we were in danger, but we could typically drive away. That was the benefit to having the car. It didn't always start, but thankfully every time I saw people who appeared to be approaching with theft—or worse—in mind, it cranked right up. That, in itself, was miraculous, though I didn't think of it like that at the time.

"Lana worked one extra-large house. We relied heavily on that job for most of our food. She had to take the car, though, since it wasn't near public transportation routes. We found a few abandoned buildings where the kids and I hid while Lana drove to work twice a week. She would park the car a few blocks away—close enough to walk without difficulty but far enough away so the family wouldn't take offense to the junk heap or ask questions about teddy bears and blankets in the back seat. Her parking spot was on the edge of a rougher neighborhood.

"One morning, the kids hadn't woken up yet, and I still waited for Lana's return. She usually arrived around midnight, so panic had settled in my chest. As the kids began to stir and I was finalizing a search plan, Lana walked in. Her hair was disheveled, and I could tell she'd been crying. While she was working, someone had stolen our mobile house.

"I leaned against the cinderblock wall of the old warehouse trying to hug my crying wife to me with my head as she buried her face in my scarred chest. She still clutched her bag, the one that contained our important papers—our marriage license, the kids' birth certificates and vaccination cards, our social security cards … all things that said we used to be part of society—and half of the money we'd been carefully saving to one day get a place of our own again. I had the other half; we decided early on it would be safer that way. Lana had experienced enough to know that nothing was permanent and anything could be taken in an instant. That's why she never let that bag out of her sight.

"From that day on, we were truly homeless."

I hang my head under the remnants of shame I feel for … everything.

"Without a car, Lana lost her best job. She continued the others, though. We dipped into our savings to buy new blankets and a few other necessities. For places to sleep, though, we had to get creative. A full year with at least a consistent enclosed place to sleep had come to an end, and we faced a second winter without even metal and glass to shield us from the bitter temperatures.

"We had to stay within walking distance of transportation or Lana's jobs. That limited us but also opened our eyes to a few homeless communities. Our first experience was terrifying.

"Soon after we entered an area where a number of people clearly called 'home,' a few of the younger men banded together. I won't repeat the words they used or the threats they made—you can fill in the gaps with your knowledge of evil. They had wicked plans for my Lana and Jenna. I could hear Lana whispering, pleading. She told me later she was praying for our children's ears and eyes to be closed, for them to not experience the atrocities being threatened, for them to be spared. All I could do was stand there and put myself between the gang and my family. Without arms to defend them, I prepared to use feet, teeth, anything I could to protect the people I loved more than life itself."

My pulse has quickened with this part of our story. I remember how everything that evening looked red. I think it was the combination of my rage and terror that colored the scene. I blink to keep it from happening again and to allow my heartbeat to slow.

"I only thought I'd been helpless before that night. We had no hope that I saw. As the men circled us with knives and chains in their hands, I prayed for the first time in my life. 'If you exist, God of the universe, now is the time to show us and defend us when we can't possibly defend ourselves.' Those were the exact words I prayed, though I have no idea where they came from. It was like I read off cue cards. Next, time stood still. The thugs around us moved in slow motion. I took several calm, deep breaths; and my whole being filled with peace, of all things.

"The men suddenly stopped. Horror distorted every face, and they ran backward as fast as they could until they turned, some falling and clawing back to standing. They ran like I've never seen, while constantly looking over their shoulders—terror ringing their eyes.

"When I turned, I didn't see anything. The air felt warm, though, and I smelled something sweet. My children sat together, holding hands and singing. They had no idea why their mama and I were so shaken up. They told us they liked this new place and asked how long we could stay. Our Jenna turned to Lana and asked, 'Aren't they amazing?'

"My wife's voice trembled as she responded, 'Aren't who amazing?'

"'The angels.' Jenna's simple response shook my entire belief system, and I began to think there might be something more to this life."

As I scan the crowd, I see no more discomfort. I see only damp faces, awe and mouthed praises.

"I spent much of my life paving my way and pulling myself up by my own bootstraps. I didn't want to rely on anyone; I was the only person my family needed. While parts of that might be admirable, I realize now that I never could do anything on my own and that we were created for community, for dependence and for leaning on each other—but most of all on God.

"Those were the concepts I was wrestling with when Jack Calhoun met us at the other homeless community a few months later. Lana and I continued to tuck away the money she made.

At that point, we were able to do it more quickly. We didn't need to buy gas anymore, and most of our food came from the community we'd joined. The day-old food and bread allowed us to take the money we would have used to survive and save it instead. We replaced the money we had to use for new supplies and crept closer to enough for a few months' rent.

"We were contemplating who to trust, where to get me the help I needed to reenter the job force and how to find an affordable place to live so our children could return to school. When Jack gave me Ducky's number, I knew God had provided again.

"God's word is right. Every good thing comes from above, and without God's good gifts, we wouldn't be here.

"Thanks to Ducky—and to all of you here at Sovereign Grace—my family has found a community and a home. Most of all, we have found a place where we can learn more about the God who I now know is real, who woke me up and rocked my self-centered world and who guarded and protected my family in our darkest days."

My heart lightens with the release of our story. God's Spirit empowers me and fills me with the knowledge that He does comfort, protect and care.

"No matter what job I'm able to do once I get prosthetic arms and learn to use them, I will find ways to give back—to others who find themselves suddenly helpless, to those who think they can control their own futures and to those who believe themselves to be islands with no need for a community like the one we've found here."

Lana and I lock eyes and smiles.

"God kept us together, despite our naivety, fear and pride. Now it's our turn to give to others in their desperate times, and we accept the challenge to always lend a hand."

As the audience rises to clap or wipe their faces, their laughter at my final pun rings full and genuine. Not bad for a kid from the country who's not much for public speaking.

Absence, Reflected

Reflecting Absence.

The couple in the hotel lobby mentioned the name. They talked about the memorial's opening. Today's ceremony is only for the family and friends who lost loved ones on 9/11, they said; so, I'm not sure why I came.

The site isn't far from my hotel, technically on my way to the meeting. Still, why am I standing outside the construction fencing, all alone, in this giant city that's never quiet?

Two cabs launch a honking match to prove my point.

I came to New York for Fashion Week, the ultimate event for a new designer, and the meeting in two hours could change my future.

And yet, here I stand.

What are the chances that my once-in-a-lifetime dream trip to New York City lands me here at the opening of this memorial on the ten-year anniversary of the attacks?

It's not like I can go in. I don't have the right to grieve here. My loss came two and a half years before theirs.

I think it's the title.

Yes. The name of the memorial drew me here.

It could describe me.

My smile, my drive, my daily determination to prove myself and to make a better life for me and little Stevie—are they simply reflections of the absence of my love? Am I no longer living, just projecting a mirror image of all I lost … *who* I lost?

Steven kissed me for the last time more than twelve years ago. Since then, I've felt empty, except for the daily rush of emotions. They cascade within me—a waterfall without end.

The memorial is a waterfall, the couple mentioned. It sinks into the ground where the Towers once stood. Those buildings must have been incredible to see in person. I only ever saw them on TV, but they seemed indestructible—solid, unmoving, eternal.

Like mine and Steven's love.

If I learned nothing else on that muggy spring night beside the old dirt road where Steven raced for the last time, I learned that nothing on earth's meant to last. Not towers, not plans, not love.

I didn't even get to tell him our news. The plan was to tell him that night when he snuck over to my house. I'd slip open my window, and we'd snuggle in my bed like we'd done many nights. His heartbeat would put me to sleep, and his kiss would wake me. Then he'd slip out and make it across the three pastures between our houses before the sun rose.

That night, I would've put my head on his chest like always and whispered, "You're gonna be a daddy."

Instead, I spent the night heaving into a toilet at the hospital because I'd watched his car flip and spin like an out-of-control top and leave our baby fatherless.

Steven would've been ecstatic. He wasn't like most guys. He wanted us to build a family together. We had talked about our future a lot. We started dating in sixth grade, and he told me after our sixth-grade graduation that he was going to put a ring on my finger one day. I told him I'd like that. Then I took his hand and let him kiss me.

He didn't get to keep that promise. His brother Jerry gave me the ring. After we said goodbye to Steven at the cemetery, Jerry told me his brother had planned to ask me at prom and handed me a palm-sized black box.

"This is yours," he said.

"This is his," I replied, my hand on my stomach.

Neither of us had tears left to spill. Jerry would've been a good uncle, but he took off after graduation. He couldn't make a life in the town where both his big brother and mom died.

Their dad didn't have much to do with me or little Stevie. I can't blame him. He tried, but Stevie looked exactly like his daddy. Mr. Goodtime saw a ghost whenever he looked at his grandson.

My parents told me I was an embarrassment and kicked me out of the house.

For a long time, I imagined how life might have been. When I closed my eyes, for a moment, Steven was there. I wore his ring, and we raised his son together. We were a family with a little house where Steven would build the white picket fence he promised me. We even had a dog.

The problem was, I always had to open my eyes. Returning to reality got harder to do, so I stopped pretending.

Could have beens don't help.

People begin to trickle out of the memorial. As they branch off around me, I recognize in some of their faces the pained look that accompanies a haunting by *could have beens*. In others, I see anger or desperation or resignation.

As I identify my emotions leaking from their faces, I bitterly decide they're reflections of me. The grief stains I view every morning in my mirror exist on these people who were left behind a decade ago to pick up their lives' debris.

No memorial will help them. Steven's gravestone sure doesn't help me. I've rubbed his name so much, it shows. No genie exists, though; he's not coming back.

Neither are their loved ones.

And so, we all wander through life: searching, seeking, missing, aching. *Reflecting Absence.*

I think about the people who helped me move on with my life and those who told me this day and this meeting would come if I believed in and worked toward my dreams.

When my parents kicked me out, I went to Rachael. Her dad was the Baptist preacher, and she was the only girl in our high school who didn't judge me or talk about me. It's not like they weren't all doing the same things with their boyfriends. I was just the one who got knocked up and planned to have our son, even if his father couldn't be with us.

Rachael was the first person I told—right after that awful crash, when I had seen Steven's bashed-in head pressed against the driver's side window and was still numb with shock. She held my hand at the funeral. And when I had nowhere else to turn, she opened her arms to me and stuck by me. She cried with me and prayed for me.

Her boyfriend had been hurt that night. In some ways, she lost him then, too. Twelve years later, though, she's got him back. She gets to wear his ring. She gets to fall into his arms again.

And, I'm so happy for her. When she called me a few days ago to tell me Jack proposed, I squealed. She is my best friend, and I want the best for her. I wipe away a tear because I am happy for her, but I can't stop the waterfall of loss in me.

Others can live. Though I have a life—and a good one, one to be thankful for—I don't know how to live. My ability to do that evaporated with Stephen's final breath.

That night shifted our town. Of our classmates who were there and didn't die, most of them left Bellum as soon as they could. The ones who stuck around pretend we haven't all been friends since kindergarten. I guess that's how they continue living.

Once our tears had dried after that night, Rachael helped me come up with a life plan. I moved in with my great-aunt and finished my junior year—the highest I'd get with school. Rachael helped me fill out job applications and prepare for interviews. I got a few jobs to help me start a bank account and work toward a future for my growing family.

Whenever I wasn't working or helping Aunt Grace around her house, I spent time with Rachael. We talked about the baby, the guys we missed and the futures we wanted. She told me she wanted to open a fitness center for women. I told her I wanted to design clothes. She couldn't believe I made all my clothes—something that came in handy when I got bigger but had no money for maternity clothes. I had never told the girls at school because they would have made fun of me for wearing homemade clothes. Only Steven had known my secret and my dream. He told me I could do it, and Rachael did too.

She and Ms. Becky, Rachael's boyfriend's mom, hosted a shower for me at Bellum Baptist Church. They got folks all over town to show up with loads and loads of diapers, clothes, fabric to make more as he grew, formula and baby gear. Before that afternoon, I didn't have anything for a baby and wasn't sure how I would manage even the essentials.

Pastor Burns and a couple of the church's deacons transported the crib, stroller, playpen, car seat, changing table and other gifts. He and Rachael helped me put together the furniture.

Once everything was assembled, Rachael handed me one more bag. She and her dad gave me a race car bedding set and a stuffed race car for little Stevie. She and I had been flipping through a baby catalog, and I burst into tears when I saw it. I told her me and Steven would have picked that out for our son.

She remembered. She also knew better than to let me open it in front of a bunch of people. That's a great friend.

The flow of people exiting the memorial slows. I peek inside. When I don't see anyone monitoring who's coming and going, I join the stragglers.

The park is bigger than I expected. When I reach the memorial and look down, it's deeper than I imagined. The water rushes over all four sides, yet the sound of its ceaseless crashing is … peaceful.

I raise my hand but pull it back before touching any of the thousands of names. I see flowers, photos, notes next to names that will never smell, see or read them. I never bring flowers to Steven's grave; it seems pointless.

When I visit him, I talk. He's had a play-by-play of our son's nearly twelve years of life, which I'm sure some would consider more pointless than a bouquet.

Little Stevie was born in October 1999. I went into labor in the middle of the night. Aunt Grace was sound asleep and couldn't drive in the dark even if she were awake. I tried to drive myself but didn't make it past getting the keys before doubling over with a contraction.

I breathed through that one and called my only friend. Rachael's dad answered as another contraction hit. He told me he and Rachael were on their way. Fifteen minutes later, they helped me stand up from the front steps and Rachael climbed in the back seat with me. She held my hand the entire drive.

It didn't occur to me before I went into labor that I would be terrified of bringing a baby into the world alone. Rachael didn't act surprised. When we got to the hospital and the nurse prepared to wheel me back, I freaked out and squeezed Rachael's hand.

"I'm too scared."

Without a blink, Rachael smiled and said, "You don't need to be; I'm not leaving you."

She didn't.

Once Stevie was a month old, I got two of my old jobs back—and we needed them. Aunt Grace wasn't in good enough health to care for a baby, so I had to pay for childcare. That's where most of my money went. Thankfully, my aunt never charged me rent and bought some of our groceries. She cooked when I was at work and made sure I ate well every day.

The following summer, Aunt Grace had a mild stroke, and I took over the cooking. By then I was doing sewing and embroidery from home, in addition to my other jobs. A few ladies learned I sewed most of Stevie's clothes and asked me to make some for their daughters. Word spread quickly and more people asked me to sew for them than I had time to handle.

Rachael came over one Saturday to help me with Stevie while I caught up on some orders for adult customers.

I asked her, "Is this all there is to life? Working in meaningless, boring jobs that pay next to nothing and leave no time to do what I'm passionate about?"

Rachael didn't roll her eyes at my complaining or laugh at my bitterness. Instead, she said, "I don't think it has to be. What would be your first step toward your dream of designing clothes full time?"

"Well, I'm not sure where to start. I need to be doing way more of this." I held up the skirt I designed to flatter my customer's shape. "To do enough, though, I'd need some machines. Hand sewing takes a lot of time."

I finished the skirt and examined it. "I'm not sure I could just design and make clothes, though. Since it would have to be my only job, I'd have to be able to pull in enough money. I could open a shop—like a boutique—and sell popular brands."

"You've got your starting point!" At my confused expression, Rachael explained. "Open a boutique."

"But, how? I don't know anything about business, and I don't have a building or money to get one. I'd also need money to buy inventory."

"Who do we know who owns a business?"

"Ms. Pam has had the hair salon for years."

"Of course! Want to talk to her after church tomorrow?" Rachael was clapping her hands, so I knew I better say yes.

"I think you're more excited than I am." I laughed as my friend danced around the living room with an oblivious baby Stevie.

"You'll be much more excited once we get some answers. You'll see—your dreams can come true!"

The only other person to believe in my dreams was Steven.

Added together, mine and Steven's grades wouldn't have got us in college. We didn't excel in the classroom. Tests and books weren't our things. His was cars; mine, design and sewing. Most people dismissed our passions and us. We weren't exactly voted Most Likely to Amount to Anything.

The things we knew, though, we really knew.

He could listen to an engine or put his hand on a car hood and know what was wrong—even when the owner didn't have a clue there was an issue. Behind the wheel, he was even more magical. He took the sharpest curves on Bellum's backroads faster than anyone.

When my parents first let me go for drives with him, he'd accelerate into turns, and I'd scream and beg him to stop. It didn't take long, though, for me to give him my heart and trust. He'd have the pedal to the floor while I sat on my knees with my head and arms outstretched from the window. Eyes closed, swallowing the wind through my smile, I heard him laughing and yelling, "That's my girl!"

I was his girl.

His absence might suck me over the edge of this memorial. How can the ache still be this intense? Shouldn't the pain have dulled by now?

Grief has taught me one thing: Love and loss have no expiration dates.

Neither do dreams.

I'm as passionate about design as I was nearly eleven years ago when I opened my boutique. Mr. Woodruff let me use one of his downtown buildings rent-free for the first four months. I had two investors who helped me buy my starting inventory and all the clothing racks and other business tools I needed.

Aunt Grace kissed my cheek and slurred out the words, "I'm proud of you and want you to have this." In my hand, she slipped a roll of hundred-dollar bills.

With their faith and support following Rachael's initial push, I opened Butterfly Kisses Boutique on Stevie's first birthday. I sold other people's designs for children's clothing and offered embroidery services. I took custom sewing orders, and demand for my designs boomed. Word got around that I had a knack for fitting the right outfit to the right body type and the right color to the right complexion. Soon, I had customers coming from five counties over for style advice.

Within six months, I'd paid back my investors and bought more machines. Within a year, I started hanging some of my own designs on the rack and filled more custom orders for adults under the label *Stevie G. Fashions.*

My achievements were all thanks to Rachael's encouragement and to the people in the community who took a chance on my passion. My success inspired my friend and me to start something in 2001 at the local rehab mission. We called it Passion Discovery.

Rachael's friend Shannon, another single teen mom, was our first participant. Her parents gave her a camera. She had a talent to use it well and a passion for photography. We helped her launch her photography business, and she had a waiting list of clients once her little girl was a month old.

The three of us helped other women in and around Bellum turn their passions into careers, and we became best friends in the process. Rachael moved to Savannah with her dad and started college near there. Shannon lives in Augusta now with her husband and daughter and travels all over doing wedding photography. People get on her waiting list years in advance and pay big bucks for her.

My designs have slowly made their way into boutiques across the South, including Savannah—thanks to Rachael. That's where a well-known designer from New York saw my clothes and invited me to fly here to meet with her and industry experts from around the world.

That meeting starts in less than an hour, but for some reason, here I am—staring at this massive hole in the ground. A hole that's not really a hole anymore. It's constantly refilling with water—an endless cycle—that reflects the sky overhead.

As I walk around the memorial's perimeter, I wonder what little Stevie would think of this place. He would find the memorial impressive, but I doubt he'd like the city. He's heard me talk about it and knows how important this opportunity is to me. If he were here, he'd make me feel sure of myself.

That's what his daddy did. Steven always made me believe I could do something big. When he died, I thought the confidence he gave me passed away too.

For our son, I had to find a way to continue life. I picture him—my sweet little Stevie, with his Daddy's eyes and hands and smooth talking. He is a living reflection of the man who will always hold my heart.

Living.

I can't just *have* a life; I must *live* it. If I'm going to honor Steven's memory, I should be a living memorial, too. That's what Steven would want. More than a gravestone or spoken updates on his son's life, he would want me to be living for our son—for him.

My determination, though rusty, spreads through me as I exit the park and continue along the crowded sidewalks to the meeting that could put Stevie G. Fashions in boutiques all over the country ... and maybe the world.

"You always said I could, Steven. I hope I make you and our son proud."

Family will always include those no longer with us. For every choice I make, goal I achieve and dream I follow, I will truly be living for him, while still *Reflecting Absence.*

Legacy
of
Sacrifice

"I thank my God, making mention of you
always in my prayers, hearing of your love
and faith which you have toward the Lord
Jesus and toward all the saints, that the
sharing of your faith may become
effective by the acknowledgment of every
good thing which is in you in Christ
Jesus. For we have great joy and consolation
in your love, because the hearts of the saints
have been refreshed by you, brother."
Philemon 4-7

In-Between Moments

It's in the mystical moments between dead asleep and wide awake, when memories resurrect, that my Edwin returns to me.

The fan's breeze caresses my face, and we're back in our living room, newlyweds dancin'—cheeks together—to the smooth lilt of Count Basie, Duke Ellington, all our favorites. I feel the side of my mouth lift in that half-smile he always teased me bout.

"Awww, Ethel, don't give me that half-moon. Shine all your radiance on me."

Modern jazz interrupts my reminiscin'. The alarm pulls me over to full wakefulness and the reminder of what today's holdin'.

Another see ya later.

I take my time risin'. It's what you do when you're 92. Test all the little things first—eyelids, pinkies, elbows, toes. If they respond, then you consider slidin' up to sittin' ... slowly. I lean against the headboard of the bed Edwin and I shared for more than seventy years. My sleep-ringed eyes land on the black dress hangin' across the room.

Today'll be my third time wearin' it. Last time was three years before, sayin' see ya later to my Edwin. First time, though, had been the double funeral.

Little Trayvon'd been a scrawny eight-year-old. It took him two years past that funeral to start shootin' up to his 6 feet, 4 inches. His parents never got to watch him grow. Gangs took 'em away. Initiations never made sense to me; made plenty of orphans.

My Trayvon had me, though; and I had him ... until now.

Today's his day.

When he earned that uniform, I knew the chance; same as when my Edwin wore his—despite the cursin' and short looks down long noses he and the other Montford Pointers suffered for their right to serve.

Yes, I knew the dangers war carries, but I didn't believe I'd be wearing black for Trayvon.

He was my baby from the first moment I laid eyes on that scrunchy face and kissed that too-big-for-him nose. A few years later, he got picked on for that nose. He came runnin' up the steps after school, eyes leakin' all over his 'rithmetic book.

"Mercy, Trayvon Edwin Henry! What on earth happened, baby?"

"All the boys in my class do is pick on me bout my big ol' nose. Why'd I have to get a honker like this one?"

"Why? To smell my sweet tater pies from miles away, of course. God knew you needed to be able to find your way home to your grandma any time you've gone too far. You'll always have a home in your grandma's arms. Now, you come over here and give me a hug, my sweet man."

Thinkin' of his teary hug that day always fogs up my eyes.

No time for tears. I toss back the quilt and sheet, swing my legs over until my feet burrow into the fluffy pink slippers—a gift from Trayvon last Christmas, before he left for Iraq. He knew how chilly my feet get and he noticed me lookin' longing-like at them in the Sears catalog.

I hit the radio's off button harder than necessary, perhaps. Today's jazz isn't the same. I always liked the music parts most of all. Edwin preferred those croonin' ladies: Blanche Calloway, Lena Horne, Billie Holiday. He'd have me sing him all his favorites whenever we rode around the countryside for him to preach.

The eggs whisk up, and I tear some sliced cheese into the foam. That's the way Trayvon liked 'em. I whisper-sing Trayvon's favorite, "Swing, Brother, Swing," and drop the sausage patties in the skillet, let 'em sizzle 'til they tell me to flip 'em.

Food talks to you—if you'll listen. I taught Trayvon that. He'd cook with me most Sundays before he deployed.

I scoop the sausage onto my plate once it's done, get those eggs scramblin' in the sausage drippin's. Yesterday, I baked my biscuits, so I warm up a couple on the lip of the pan as I stir, stir, scrape; stir, stir, scrape. The best food demands the most attention. I slide those eggs, set just right, out by the sausage, turn down my burner and let my biscuits warm a moment more while I get my butter and jelly ready to paint inside 'em.

Feels wrong to be eatin'. If I decided not to eat any time my heart hurt or loneliness draped me like a heavy, itchy shawl ... well, I don't reckon I'd have eaten much over the years. Specially round the times I have to shimmy my way in that black gown, hangin' up, waitin' on me. It might be in the other room, but I feel its presence, hoverin'.

I chew through the food and memories.

For most of his childhood, Trayvon'd carried this chocolate-colored bear in Marine dress blues. He held it tightest when we were learnin' to say see ya later to his sweet mama and daddy.

The day of the service, that raggedy bear lost his way somewhere in the funeral home. Lots of services that day. More'n Sam, the director, liked to pack into a day. I called him up and told him bout the bear. I told him I knew he was busy and understood if it took a while.

That man says back to me, "Now, Grandma Ethel, ain't nuthin' more important to me right now than gettin' that boy back his bear. You just fix him his favorite pie, and I'll be by later."

Sure 'nough, near dusk-time, here he comes—suit, tie and a big ol' oil stain across it all. He'd army-crawled behind some old hearses in their garage to keep his promise. "No bear left behind, ma'am," he'd told me.

That same sweet man let me cry on his shoulder yesterday as we discussed the honor guard for my Trayvon.

I wasn't the only one cryin', though.

That's somethin' bout folks—they care and they see. Even when you don't notice, others are watchin' you, learnin' from you and findin' hope or inspiration or joy in the watchin'. It's a beautiful sight to behold. Lots of times we miss it—until we're layin' a loved one down to rest.

I finish my chewin' and clean away the dishes 'fore I get myself ready. As I work my way into that black dress, I catch myself hatin' it. I remind myself that, while the loss might be sad for me now, it shows me hope. Hope for eternity ahead; eternity now for my Edwin, my Marcus and Maggie—he called her his Magpie—and now for my Trayvon.

They're livin' their eternities out now up on those golden streets, dancin' together with my Jesus. I smile as I smooth a wrinkle in the skirt and ignore the ones on my face. One day

I'll be up there, too, dancin' on those sparkly streets—no more black dresses … or wrinkles.

Sam'll be by soon. He told me yesterday—once we'd both used up some tissues—that he'd pick me up personally in his fancy funeral home car to drive me to the cemetery. I knew my Trayvon loved outside too much to keep him stuck inside a stuffy chapel. We'll remember him in the great outdoors, but first I'll see his face one last time.

True to his word, Sam taps on my door at 9:45.

"You ready, Grandma Ethel?"

"No. But, I'm makin' my steps anyway."

The whole ride I sift through my mind the people who'll be there—like sifting flour for my biscuits. As I do, I cut prayers into my thinking, like ice-cold butter in the dough.

I'll see Lewan and Eli from the center. Trayvon played ball with them, and those boys had looked up to him since they were no bigger than the shrubs round the funeral home. Lewan'll be in his dress blues. He followed my Trayvon's footsteps. I'm prayin' he won't get sent over to that desert too. He's nearby at Lejeune, still trainin'—safer now than he could be.

Bring these boys to you, dear Jesus. Make them men after your heart to follow and serve you, leadin' others as they do. Just like my Trayvon.

I grin as I think of sweet Tiffanee. She and Trayvon'd been as stuck on each other as two young'uns could be. He'd been wise past his years when he told her they'd have to part ways, though. He knew it didn't matter how many butterflies she gave him, he couldn't become one flesh with a girl who didn't serve his Jesus.

They'd both worn their broken hearts on their sleeves … and faces … long after their split. I don't believe either one ever stopped the pinin', though. I know she'll be there today, and I'll hold her long as she'll let me. She lost her grandma and mama too young. All she has are them aunts; and they ain't worth the havin', I'm afraid.

Trayvon showed her another way—your way, Lord. Help her take hold of it and break that mold the women in her family got stuck in.

Reggie'll be there—the world's weight restin' between his shoulder blades. That man! Never could move past not catchin' the children playin' tough guns who shot down Marcus and Maggie. He visited us all the time as Trayvon grew. He'd toss the ball or talk sports. Don't know that I've ever seen him smile, though. Don't reckon I'll see one on him today neither.

Lift that burden up off his shoulders, Lord Jesus. That man ain't to blame, but he needs to know that truth. And, he needs to know You.

Then there'll be Jack and his mama, Becky. He's fresh outta the hospital from the same attack that took our Trayvon. She called and talked to me a long time last night. Jack's clutchin' the blame he put on himself for Trayvon's death. He's done that an awful lot in his short life.

So many burdens, my Jesus! Lift Jack's today, too. Give him peace and help him forgive himself. You know how guilt festers, grows, spreads in a person—worse than cancer. Cut that mess outta him. You're the best surgeon of all, so I know you can. Wrap your arms around his sweet mama and put the right words in her mouth to speak your truth to her boy.

Sam parks beneath the canopy to the family entrance at the funeral home. I mentally rehearse the next steps. We'll walk in and I'll say my see ya later to Trayvon before the guard carries him out to his car. We'll make a small procession down the windy road to the cemetery.

None of this feels real—certainly not right. There's nothin' natural bout layin' a grandson to rest and then walkin' on, livin' life.

In the time Sam takes to walk around this car, open my door and lead me by the hand, I pray again for each one comin' today to honor my Trayvon. I pray for their smiles to shine through the sorrow, but more'n that, I pray for their souls. It's what Trayvon always prayed for, and I'll keep doin' that for him.

I know Trayvon's body left behind isn't him. He's alive and well with our Savior. Seein' him laid out there in his snappy dress blues, I clutch my hands to my chest. My heart beats out the Marines' Hymn. Both my Edwin and Trayvon stood straighter whenever they heard that song. They were proud to be Marines. No other military branch would do for them. Few and proud, they had to be. And, they were.

My prayers come whispered in spurts, disjointed like the heaving of my heart.

"Thank you for the gift my Trayvon was to me. To others. To his country." I notice the flag they'll drape over his coffin.

An honor.

From a young age, he'd always tear up whenever he covered his heart and listened to "The Star-Spangled Banner." Proud of his country, ready to defend her.

"Give me strength, my Jesus! Strength to make it through this day."

My knees don't feel as strong as I'd like 'em to be.

"Use him—his life, the words he spoke and lived—use them even now for all those comin' to remember him. All he wanted in this life was for those around him to see You. Come to you. Let today be their day of rejoicing."

Time eases past until it comes to the next steps of the day's events. I shuffle alongside Sam back to the car. We're followed now by my sweet boy, all ready to be bid farewell. Sam pulls the wrong way out of the lot. I cut my eyes at him, but he just says, "You'll see."

We make a few turns before we near the main street. Two police cars, lights flashin', wait for us. My heart thumps harder as we pull in behind one of the officers, and I wonder what on earth Sam's cooked up.

He honks and waves. The officer hits his siren with one loud wail and then pulls out alongside the other cruiser, which I now see has traffic halted. We follow onto the road, and I lose the tears I'd been holdin'.

Lined five or six rows deep on both sides, folks wave American flags. Men hold hats over their hearts. Ladies've got tears streamin'. Kids are standin' solemn; some tuggin' on their parents' sleeves, askin' the questions we all do durin' wartime.

"Well, I never …."

Sam eases another tissue into the hand restin' in my lap, and I replace my soggy one.

"I wish Trayvon could see all these folks. He'd be out here, throwin' footballs to these kids and wavin' flags with all these sweet, sweet people."

My voice breaks under the pang of missin' his smilin' face. Another officer waits where we'll turn once more at the end of this main stretch. Cars stretch far behind him, and I recognize many of them: Eli and Lewan, Tiffanee, others.

Lights on. Sunglasses down. Tissues wipin' at their emotions. I dab at mine, too.

We snake on around the cemetery's slippery roads to the tent set up for my precious boy. A fragrant privacy fence of flowers surrounds the chairs waitin' on us.

Sam helps me get seated and fusses over me like I know my Edwin, Marcus and Trayvon would have done … had they been here.

Once the rustlin' of people behind me settles, our preacher steps in front. He stands by Trayvon's coffin that the guard had carried in and saluted. He looks down at it a moment before startin' to speak.

"Before he shipped out, Trayvon and me sat down and talked about this day. He knew we might be here together without him and made one request. I promised him I'd grant it. So … we're gonna have some church up in here today. Amen?"

"Amen!" I hear the chorus behind me as I imagine that conversation with our Rev. Williams and laugh at my Trayvon's request.

The preacher launches a presentation of the Gospel that lays down the truth of God's word and His one way to salvation. I can hear my Trayvon givin' up his *Amens* all the way through and smile as I picture him havin' church up in heaven with our family round that big ol' throne.

I look behind me, and I'm seein' tears and changin' faces. So, I start up the prayin' again. Tiffanee looks like she stuck her face in the water hose like she and Trayvon used to do on hot summer days. She's got her hands clasped before her mouth, but I see her lips movin'. "Praise Jesus!"

Praise Jesus!

Lewan's down on one knee in his dress blues, and I know he's prayin'.

Lord, give him that faith he needs. Bring your lamb on home to the fold. Praise you, my Jesus!

Eli's fidgetin'. And, have mercy! Reggie—usually solid as stone—the moisture on his cheeks sparkles in the sunlight, and I see a liftin' of the burden on his shoulders and of the anger in those steely eyes.

Break 'em down and bring 'em to you! Praise Jesus!

Jack's at attention, still in the guard of Marines there to honor Trayvon. He's got that Marine frown etched on, but I see his eyes—painfilled, haunted, achin'. I see the way his mama's watchin' him and want to hug 'em both to me and pass on all the love I got to give.

I don't always have the right prayin' words. Good thing my God knows what they are. I give Jack up to Him and join in the final shout of "Amen!"

The Marines fold up the flag that had draped Trayvon's casket. Such neatness, done so careful. Now, it's just Jack. He's holdin' it carefully; he's only got the one good arm now. He turns, sharp as can be, to march it up to me. I watch that jaw of his clench and set as he pushes something back down deep ... somethin' I almost saw in those golden flecks that flash in his eyes. He's passin' me the flag, and I feel his anguish clinging to each memorized word:

"On behalf of the President of the United States, the Commandant of the Marine Corps and a grateful nation, please accept this flag as a symbol of our appreciation for your grandson's service to Country and Corps."

I don't want to but I'm blubberin'. Tears or not, I got to say somethin'. I grab Jack's good hand and hoist myself up. I wrap that sweet boy—so like my own grandson—in a big ol' hug and whisper past my cryin', "You got to forgive yourself, my sweet Jack. You got to forgive, let go that grief and guilt and *live. Live* for our Trayvon. You know that's what he'd want. All he ever wanted was for you to live now and live forever. I pray ev'ry day he'll see you again in heaven."

Jack presses a gentle kiss to my old weepy cheek as I clutch his hand tight. I see him crumblin', and I pray harder—claimin' what I believe God's gonna do one day.

You're gonna save this baby one day. I know you are, so I'm gonna praise you right now for that, Lord Jesus.

One by one, folks pass by. They share stories and give hugs. Jack's mama comes by, and I give her a big ol' bear hug.

"I'm so glad God chose you to mama that sweet boy of yours. You know I pray for you—and him—ev'ry day. I ask God to remind you He gave you ev'rything you need to mother that stubborn young man. And, I'm believin' our God's gonna save him."

"You sound just like my best friend, Carolina." Becky's smile lights up her face, and I give her another squeeze. "Thank you for the prayers. We just have to keep praying and believing, don't we?"

"That's the very best we can do, honey!"

Reggie bends down next for a hug. "Grandma Ethel."

"Please tell me I'm gonna see you at the church this week."

He surprises me with a hint of a smile. "If you bake me one of your sweet potato pies, I might just sit right by you."

"I'll bake you two."

"Done!" He walks off with a creaky chuckle followin' after him. I reckon I'll never stop bein' surprised at folks.

I see Tiffanee's been waitin', and I pull up the new box of tissues Sam's brought over. "Get on over here, baby girl."

She laughs despite her grief, and we sit.

"Grandma Ethel, I gave my heart to Jesus today, and I'm happy but I'm so damn mad. If I'd done this years ago, I coulda been Tray's girl."

I hand over the tissues and wrap my arms around her. "You were always Trayvon's girl. And now, that boy of ours is dancin' round with Jesus, celebratin' you and prob'ly yellin' 'Tiff-y-nee!!' at the top of his mighty lungs."

Laughter heals in times of grief; so, we do more healin'. She shares stories I never knew, and I tell her bout Trayvon's letters from Iraq and his friend Jack. We arrange for her to come over and learn to make pie crusts next Saturday.

"I plan on spendin' more time with you. I don't want you to be lonely. Maybe I'm a little lonely too sometimes." She looks down at the balled-up tissue. "And, I might need some help figurin' out this God thing."

"My door's always open—night and day!"

I cover her hands in mine and pray for her and then watch her walk toward her car. She turns and waves, like I knew she'd do. I wave back and pray again.

Praise you, Jesus!

"Get on over here, you rascal." I turn and point at Lewan. He's been mischievous since the day he was born, and I don't reckon he'll ever not be.

He gives me that up-to-somethin' grin that usually earns him a swat from my wooden spoon and a plate of whatever's comin' outta my oven.

"Grandma Ethel, you get prettier ev'ry time I see you; you know that, right?"

"And, you don't get any better at lyin'." I purse my lips at him but break down and laugh as I hug his neck. He hugs me back, then pulls away and takes my hands in his.

His expression sobers. "You know, Tray started writin' me when I went to Boot Camp. We wrote while he was in Iraq, too. He'd always share somethin' from the Bible, but it never felt preachy. Anyway, he got me thinkin' and askin' questions. I wanted to talk to him in person about some stuff, but Rev. Williams brought the answers today. I prayed."

"Well, praise Jesus!" The tears flow again, but I'm too happy to care. I know my Trayvon's singin' with the angels, and I close my eyes to imagine what that choir sounds like.

Lewan and Eli promise to see me at church Sunday, and Sam takes my arm to lead me back to the car.

I stop by the casket. Hand on top, I whisper, "Look at all you did with your one short life, baby boy. You've got a whole host comin' up to join you one day, and I can't wait to be there, too. Until then, I'll see you in the in-between moments. Ask your grandpa; he'll tell you all bout 'em. See ya later, my handsome boy."

Resources

Within the pages of this fictional account, you'll find much truth in the pain and struggles of our main character. For that reason, we have included a list with some resources in the United States for your own battles and beasts. For more local guidance and assistance, contact a church near you. Help awaits, friend. Accept it!

SUICIDE PREVENTION: 1-800-273-8255

suicidepreventionlifeline.org

SUBSTANCE ABUSE: 1-888-633-3239

http://drughelpline.org

HOMELESSNESS: 211

www.211.org/services/housing-and-utilities

PTSD & OTHER VETERAN-SPECIFIC CHALLENGES: 211

www.woundedwarriorproject.org

TO REPORT A TRAFFICKING SITUATION: 1-888-373-7888, 233733 (text)

www.humantraffickinghotline.org/chat

TO REPORT MISSING CHILDREN OR CHILD PORNOGRAPHY: 1-800-THE-LOST (843-5678)

www.report.cybertip.org

Credits & Sources

First, I extend my gratitude, appreciation and respect to several professionals who freely gave of their time to guide my research and answer specific questions paper and ink research couldn't address.

Thank you to **Edward G. Lengel,** former Senior Director of Programs at the National WWII Museum in New Orleans and current Chief Historian at the National Medal of Honor Museum, for pointing me in the best direction for my Montford Point Marine questions.

Deepest gratitude to **Dr. Charles Neimeyer,** LtCol/USMC (ret.), Director of Marine Corps History and the Gray Research Center at Marine Corps University, Quantico, Virginia, for his outstanding answers to my questions about the Montford Point Marines and for the additional, vital research recommendations.

For the second book in a row, **Gareth Minton,** Licensing & Intellectual Property Coordinator for David Austin Roses Ltd, graciously granted me permission to mention the 'L.D. Braithwaite' rose variety. His permission extended from the first book to the short story I didn't know would come later, and he directed me to another rose expert to handle specific questions.

Last, but not least, gramercy to **Rebecca Koraytem,** U. S. Sales Executive with David Austin Roses Ltd, for her knowledgeable and vital answers to my final rose-related questions. Any inaccuracies in my depiction of rose care result from my ignorance or creative license.

Primary Sources

While the totality of my research far exceeds the following, these are a few of the primary sources I used during the research, writing and revisions of *Every Good Thing*.

The Marines of Montford Point: America's First Black Marines
Melton A. McLaurin

Right to Fight: African-American Marines in WWII
Bernard C. Nalty

Blacks in the Marine Corps
The History and Museums Division, Headquarters, U.S. Marine Corps, Washington, D.C.

History of U.S. Marine Corps Operations in World War II, Volumes I-V
The Historical Branch, G-3 Division, Headquarters, U.S. Marine Corps
(The collection totals 3,631 pages of invaluable detailed accounts of every battle and movement, including the complicated logistics of wartime.)

The National WWII Museum in New Orleans, LA, and online

The USS Alabama battleship in Mobile, AL

Various pages on Marines.mil, the official website of the United States Marine Corps

Various JSTOR articles, thanks to my fabulous local library, the St. Tammany Parish Library System

Acknowledgments

The act of writing might be solitary; but the best books rest on shelves, in great part, thanks to the people who surround and uplift their authors. These are my people.

My husband, **Tony**, reminds me of my "why" when I lose focus, helps my stories remain true to me and to my characters and urges me to keep writing words because he believes they're worthy.

My children not only understand and accept the demands of deadlines but also encourage me to keep doing this crazy thing and remind me of the most important things.

My mother-in-law, **Lori Rancatore**, deserves an overdue word of thanks for graciously allowing me to turn her home into a photo studio on multiple occasions (even when she thinks things look a mess), attending and making snacks for my book signings and watching the kids when I need to work or have an event. Thanks to my father-in-law, Tony Rancatore Sr., for patiently answering many more woodshop questions and helping me brainstorm appropriate ages for the projects in "Life Lessons in Courage & Woodworking."

My critique partners, **Mea Smith** and **Kelsey Atkins**, deserve recognition for any good things in these pages. Without their suggestions, motivation, advice and brainstorming, this book wouldn't be what it is today. I'm thankful for their friendship, their truth in love, their prayers and their incredible creative minds.

My special critiquer, **Stacie Eirich**, added more depth and clarity to a story or two; and my beta readers **Terri Sweetland, Justin Stodghill, Gabrielle Hill** and **Eric Demmer** gave freely of their time to read the earlier stages and give their honest feedback. They all pushed me to fix rough patches and address prickly places that I can be stubborn about. Their love for my characters and their stories bolstered my determination to share *Every Good Thing* with readers everywhere. So, fearless readers, are you up for one more book?

My cover designer and formatter and dear friend, **Rachael Ritchey,** not only has amazing design skills but also overflows with kindness and affirmation. She often shares scripture, prayers and wise words that soothe my soul and heart and encourage my aspirations.

My **readers** make a little girl's giant dream a reality. You are why I will continue writing, creating, dreaming and publishing.

All glory to my **Creator**—the Author of the greatest story of all and the Giver of creative talents. Every Good Thing comes from Him and for Him may this book go out. Soli Deo Gloria.

My prayer for these stories is that they enlighten, inspire and edify my readers. In fiction, I pray we see the hope, light, faith and joy we need to infuse into our real world. Let us rise up from these pages and be that force. Like Ducky, may we "be the good."

The main typeface used with gracious permission in the cover design and throughout the book is Bentham, created by designer and developer, Ben Weiner. Interior formatting is primarily 12-point sizing. Headings and subheads fluctuate between 16- and 36-point sizing. For more on this typeface, read the creator's description:

"I like the lettering on nineteenth-century maps, on gravestones and on the maker's plates of cast-iron machinery. It is characterised by expressive flowing and bulging curves, mannered awkwardness and the bobbles on the terminals of its characters. The letterform conventionally called 'modern face' is the typographical equivalent, and it can be found in books printed throughout the nineteenth century. Its descendants survived into educational textbooks produced into the late twentieth century, and it is preserved in computer science as the style which Donald Knuth adopted for his TeX typesetting system.

"Bentham is a half-way design; it's true neither to the type produced during the nineteenth century, nor to the letterforms of cartographers, stonecutters, or engravers. It's really a sort of examination of the characteristics these letters share, coloured by my approach to type drawing."

The Legacy Section headers, front and back matter headers are styled in the lovely open-source Allura font by Robert Leuschke. Other fonts are Odstemplik, an open-source font by GLUK Fonts, used for the letters to Mabel, and the old news headlines use Sailors font by Amptypes (embedded by my book designer in the print version only).

Photo: Casie Jones Photography

Legacy and identity, founded on hope-filled faith, infuse the tales of the soul written from the heart of **JOY E. RANCATORE.** Her Carolina's Legacy Collection embraces everyday moments that constitute a lifetime and its heritage. Told around multiple related characters, this collection explores faith, life, death and the demons within through four mediums—novel, novella, short stories and epistolary.

An avid reader, student of human behaviors and unwitting empath, Joy absorbs emotions and spills them onto the pages of her work. Joy's technical background includes more than two decades of professional writing and editing. Ongoing training in writing, publishing, business and counseling enables her to package soul-filled stories for her readers. An award-winning, multi-genre Indie Author, Joy believes extraordinary things await her characters and their tales.

Despite a fondness for her roles as author, editor, podcaster and speaker, Joy is a hobbit at heart with Bilbo's zeal for mountains. She enjoys a life of quiet stillness with her husband, two children, dog and cat and more books than she's willing to count. When daily homeschool lessons are complete, she eagerly prepares for teatime before writing your next favorite story.

Visit Joy for Book News, Free Stories, Book
Club Kits and More:
www.joyerancatore.com/links

Have a Book Club?

READ:

Any Good Thing
(or any book in Carolina's Legacy Collection)
together.

REQUEST:

- a Book Club Kit
- a virtual or in-person chat with the author

VISIT:

www.joyerancatore.com/book-clubs

Did You Enjoy This Book?

Reviews from readers make the most precious gift for authors and help fellow readers discover fantastic new reads. Please take a moment to leave a simple star review or a few thoughts on Goodreads and any bookseller sites.

Another way to share your appreciation is to tell all your reader friends and request that your local bookstore and library shelve it.

Share your reviews and book selfies with Joy and Logos & Mythos Press on your favorite social media outlets. #AnyGoodThing

Every good Thing

JOY E. RANCATORE

Want More?

For more information on upcoming releases from
LOGOS & MYTHOS PRESS

Visit logosandmythospress.com/links and subscribe to their
email list.

Thank you for reading!

LOGOS & MYTHOS PRESS
SLIDELL, LA, USA